John Imrie

Sacred songs, sonnets and miscellaneous poems

John Imrie

Sacred songs, sonnets and miscellaneous poems

ISBN/EAN: 9783337175900

Printed in Europe, USA, Canada, Australia, Japan

Cover: Foto ©Andreas Hilbeck / pixelio.de

More available books at **www.hansebooks.com**

TO MY FRIENDS.

Friends dead and gone—friends far and near—
Friends tried and true—friends ever dear—
Though sundered far, yet all are here—
    Close to my heart;
And all along life's rugged way,
The smile of Friendship crowns the day,
And hearts are young, tho' heads be grey;
    Friends never part!

Yours truly,

John Imrie.

SACRED SONGS,

SONNETS,

AND

MISCELLANEOUS POEMS

BY

JOHN IMRIE.

WITH AN INTRODUCTION BY

G. MERCER ADAM, Toronto.

$1.00.

TORONTO:

IMRIE & GRAHAM, 28 Colborne Street.

1886.

CONTENTS.

—

LIST OF

MUSIC AND ILLUSTRATIONS.

———

MUSIC.

———

ILLUSTRATIONS.

AUTHOR'S PREFACE.

THE following "Sacred Songs, Sonnets, and Miscellaneous Poems" are sent forth to the public with much diffidence on the part of the Author as to their literary merit. I would not have dared thus to intrude on the debatable ground of authorship, unless at the urgent solicitation of my numerous friends, who have from time to time asked me for copies of some of the following compositions. At their request, also, it is gratifying to me to say, that most of the Poems have at various times appeared as contributions to the public press, more especially in Toronto, and have afterwards been copied in exchanges over Canada, and in some of the leading city papers and publications in the United States and the Mother-country. To these sources of communication with other lands and people, I tender my sincere thanks, as they have been largely instrumental in bringing my verses and my name before the public, and in stimulating me to proceed in a path—even under these auspicious circumstances—beset with much misgiving.

The Illustrations which appear in this work have been kindly supplied by friends in the printing profession ; and the Copyright Music by gentlemen whose names stand high in the scale of musical authorship.   To these, individually, my sincere thanks are hereby tendered.

My only object and aim in " the cultivation of the Muse " was to spend my leisure hours—which were all too few—in intellectual recreation, thereby giving voice to pent-up feelings of devotion, love, patriotism, or pleasure, as the " ebb and flow " of inward thought seemed to find expression. Should I thereby have " made friends " of the public, the result will far exceed my most sanguine expectations :—

> The friendship of the good and true
>   Is more to me than gold,
> And while I welcome one that's new
>   I'll treasure well the old ;
> Old friends are like the goodly tree
>   Whose leafy branches throw
> A grateful shelter over me
>   When adverse winds may blow !

TORONTO, CANADA,
   Oct. 21st, 1836.

INTRODUCTION

BY

G. MERCER ADAM.

AMONG the diverse interests of this restless money-grubbing world, there is one which should hold a larger place than it does in the affections of the masses,—namely, the honest, unaffected love of home and home pleasures. In these days we are all of us too much disposed to seek enjoyment abroad, and to figure more than is good for us in the eye of the public. The craving for excitement has made us impatient with home; and the fireside and domestic shrines have in large measure lost their attraction. In their place have come the club and the society hall, the tavern and the divorce court.

Living a fast life—the delirium which comes of it makes us impatient also with many of the simple joys which used to please a former generation. Our tastes, in these latter days, have undergone a radical change. We are fastidious and critical, and the things that once interested us and made for our peace, interest us and make for our peace no longer. In our feverish, unhealthful condition, we seek a seasoned diet; and in our reading, as well as in our eating and drinking, there is a craving for stimulants. The result is a vitiated palate, and a mind relaxed, feeble, and jaded.

We are no longer satisfied with the novel, with the song, or with the play, that used to delight our forefathers. Nothing so simple and innocent would now content us. Even our religion has suffered a change. The stern morality and unbending creeds of other days have become pliant and yielding, while compromise and emasculated beliefs have taken their place. The old doctrines familiar to the bye-gone pulpit now offend us, though we are not particular if the preacher resorts to irreverence and slang. On the contrary, we rather encourage him in this propensity.

With tastes and cravings so destructive to the

spiritual life, what wonder that simple joys and quiet domestic pleasures have in the social world lost much of their charm ? Yet "the common people,"—as the phrase goes—the men and women who are doing the common work of this toiling world, stand more than ever in need of rest and quiet, and the kindly solacement of happy fireside intercourse. Innocent delights, restful pleasures, and the blissful contentment of a well-ordered, comfortable home, with such intellectual recreation as these Edens afford, must be the necessities, we should think, of those at least whose lot is a ceaseless round of toil. To such our author comes with his tuneful lyre and sings us the gladsome lays of the home and the fireside. Benefactor is he not, to you and to me, if he beguiles us from our distractions and cares, and leads us to realize that after all the world's happiness lies in the quiet comforts and the refining influences of home ?

Neither I nor the author claim place for these effusions among the productions of the divine songsters of earth. The world has become too refined—too finical, perhaps,—in its tastes to rate highly the lays of the home, or to see aught of art in the product of the domestic Muse. But as these poems are for the people, and not for the critics, and as they deal with subjects which may be read and understood of all men,—with no artificiality, no straining after effect,—their simple and natural poetic utterance will, I am convinced, commend them to the heart, and ensure their warm acceptance at the hands of the people.

It would indeed be difficult for thoughts, however expressed, on Love, Friendship, Home, and kindred topics, to fail of finding response in the human breast; and the average reader who follows the bent of his own unperverted taste, and is as indifferent to the critics as the poets themselves, will find much to please him in the book. Of profit he should also find much, if his sympathies are as keen and broad as the author's, and his appreciation equal to his, of the warm-hearted Christian brotherhood, and unaffected moral purpose, which should find expression in all our work.

Not its least merit, it must be said, is the fact, that there is not a puzzling cr baffling line in the book. This should be counted for something, when there is so much in our modern verse, not ambitious of fame merely, but cold, meaningless and empty. The volume is chiefly noteworthy, however, not only for unassuming sincerity, on the part of the writer, but for its appeal to the universal and easily-awakened feelings of our common humanity. The unobtrusive piety and strain of religious sentiment which run, like threads of gold, through the book, will, we are sure, not the less endear the volume to the reverent reader, and to those whose hearts have felt the influences of the Divine.

May it be its mission to keep alive the love of home, to minister to minds distraught with toil and care, and among its readers—we trust, of all ranks and conditions of men—to implant an eternal Sabbath in the heart.

184 Spadina Avenue,
     Toronto, Oct. 18th, 1886.

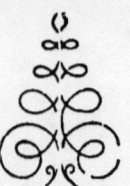

SACRED COMPOSITIONS.

Sacred Compositions.

A PRAYER.

LOWLY and prostrate,
  Kneeling before Thee,
Craving the spirit of prayer;
  Wretched and lonely,
  Seeking Thee only,
Leave me not now in despair.

  Father of mercies,
  And God of all might,
Hear Thou the sigh of my heart;
  Groping through darkness,
  Yet seeking the light,
Pardon and peace now impart.

  Oh! to be nothing,
  And Christ to be all,
Oh! to be ransomed by Thee;
  Saved from destruction
  And pow'r of the fall,
Through Jesus, who died for me.

  Humbly I ask Thee,
  Jesus, my Saviour,
Bend Thou Thine ear to my cry;
  For strength and for grace
  While running life's race—
Lead Thou me on till I die!

B

AN ANXIOUS SOUL COMFORTED.

POOR erring soul! thou art not yet forsaken,
 A Father's loving heart still beats for thee;
Renounce the steps in sin which thou hast taken,
 And thou shalt have a pardon full and free.

Let not the sins of former days deter
 Thy heart from seeking after truth and God;
Thou shalt not seek in vain, do not defer,
 Fly to the Cross, and Christ shall ease thy load.

A Father's arms are opened to receive,
 A Saviour's blood was freely shed for thee;
Trust not thy erring self, in Him believe,
 Who bore thy sins upon the cursèd tree.

No more in darkness shalt thou doubting tread,
 A brighter Light shall guide thee on thy way;
No more in sin shalt thou be blindly led,
 Nor in the paths of vice be found to stray.

Thy soul shall then in glorious measure feel
 The Spirit's power, which changes mind and will:
And thou shalt not be able to conceal
 The love which thy enraptur'd soul shall fill.

Then shalt thou grow in grace from day to day,
 And thus be fitted for thy home above;
Till God shall call thy ransom'd soul away
 To swell the praises of His matchless love.

SABBATH CHIMES.

ON HEARING THE BELLS OF ST. JAMES'S CHURCH, TORONTO,
ON A SUNDAY MORNING.

DINGLE, dingle, dong,
Hear the happy song,
 Come away,
 Sabbath day,
Join the holy throng.

Come both old and young,
Come the weak or strong,
 Dingle dong,
 Happy song,
Cheering us along.

Children young and fair,
Seeking God in prayer,
 Voices raise,
 In His praise,
Feeling God is there.

Plainly all may see,
Happy hearts have we,
 God above,
 Full of love,
Keep us near to Thee.

THE PREACHER'S WARNING.

REMEMBER, O youth! in thy early prime,
The God of thy fathers in olden time :
The Creator of heaven, and earth, and spheres,
With whom one day is as a thousand years ;
While the years of man are as early grass,
To-day in health, but to-morrow doth pass
In natural course of decay away.
To mingle again with its mother—Clay !

Ere the evil days come and years draw nigh,
When pleasure and hope give way to a sigh ;
And the eye whose lustre was clear and bright,
Gives forth but a dim and uncertain light ;
And the step, once firm and lithe in the dance,
Be crippled, and weak, and slow to advance ;
Oh ! young man, beware, and remember now
Thy Creator—God, and thy father's vow !

Let faith and prayer like daily incense rise
To God above, beyond the starry skies ;
Seek wisdom from on high as daily food,
Let not thy left hand mar thy right hand's good ;
But grow in grace, and in the knowledge rare
Which maketh rich, and Christ's atonement share ;
Then shall thy path be as the rising sun,
And God at last shall say—*Well done, well done !*

JESUS' LOVE.

OH, wondrous love! oh, matchless grace!
That Jesus took the sinner's place;
And left His heavenly home on high,
On earth to *live*, to *weep*, to *die*.

To live on earth that we might rise
To brighter scenes beyond the skies;
And dwell in mansions fair and bright,
'Mid endless glory, love, and light.

To weep, that we might sing for joy,
And all our ransom'd powers employ;
Our hearts and voices gladly raise
In happy songs of love and praise.

To die, that we might never die,
But live with Him in bliss on high;
And meet around that glorious throne,
Where Jesus gathers in His own.

The love of Jesus, like the sea,
Is rich and boundless, full and free;
No seeking soul need e'er despair,
Or fail to find a portion there.

THE BELIEVER'S REFUGE.

'TIS sweet to feel that God is near
   In times of trouble or distress,—
To quell the doubt, or calm the fear,
   To pardon, comfort, heal and bless.

When all around is dark and drear,
   And sorrow shades the brow with care,
How sweet to know that God will hear
   The anxious soul's imploring prayer.

How sweet to lean upon that arm,
   And in its strength a refuge find ;
Secure from every fear or harm,
   Which would disturb our peace of mind.

Jesus, thou Refuge ever sure,
   Where all is peace, and joy, and rest ;
Safe as the rock that doth endure,
   Oh ! let me lean upon Thy breast.

Then let the world its warfare wage,
   And Satan tempt my heart with pride ;
Let friends disown, and scoffers rage,
   To turn my heart from Thee aside—

They all shall fail ! but Thou alone
   Shalt be my portion evermore ;
I'll cling to Thee—the world disown—
   Thy love confess—and Thee adore !

THE MISSIONARY'S PRAYER.

LORD, with thine arm support our cause,
While, in obedience to thy laws,
We raise Thy banner, plead Thy pow'r,
To save when in the trying hour.

Lord, send Thy soldiers to the field,
And make the pow'rs of Satan yield
To thy strong arm, that arm of might,
Which shieldeth those who do the right.

Lord, put Thy Word into our heart,
That we to others may impart
The knowledge of Thy saving grace,
To every tribe of every race!

Then shall we praise Thy mighty name,
And in all lands Thy right proclaim;
Where prayers of gratitude will rise,
Like grateful incense to the skies.

THE CHRISTIAN'S HOPE.

WE cannot meet with undimm'd eye
   The sun's effulgent, piercing rays;
No more can we, while 'neath the sky,
   Fathom our great Creator's ways.

Still let us search, with humble awe,
   And scan His wondrous works with care ;
And round His glorious footstool draw
   In humble, pleading, fervent prayer :

That He who rules celestial spheres,
   And holds the oceans in His hand,
Would free our hearts from doubts and fears,
   And lead us to that glorious land,

Where doubts no more disturb the mind,
   And fears no more distress the heart ;
Where we shall full fruition find,
   And kindred meet no more to part.

Oh ! may we stand on heavenly ground,
   Where sweetest music charms the ear ;
Where peace, and joy, and love abound—
   For God Himself is ever near.

Oh ! glorious land of endless day,
   Oh ! happy home so bright and fair ;
Where saints unceasing homage pay
   To Him whose blood has brought them there.

THY CHOICE — WHICH ?

OH! which shall I choose,
    Accept, or refuse,—
The pleasures of sin for a season?
    Or cling to the Cross,
    Through profit or loss,
Oh! tell me, and give me a reason?

    The reasons I give
    All others outlive,—
The pleasures of sin are deceiving;
    And soon pass away,
    Like winter's short day,
And leave the soul dark with its grieving:

    Then cling to the Cross,
    And count it not loss .
To sacrifice earth's empty pleasure;
    Think nothing of pain,
    If Heaven then gain,
And there have thy storehouse of treasure!

MY PORTION.

THE Lord is my portion, then what need I
fear?
Though foes gather round me, my Helper is near;
Let troubles assail me, or dark storms arise,
I'm safe on the "Strong Tower" that points to
     the skies.

The Lord is my portion, the Lord is my Friend,
My hope from beginning, my joy in the end;
No other His place in my heart can supply,
Which wells with its fulness when Jesus is nigh.

The Lord is my portion in life and in death,
In lisping His name I shall spend my last breath,
For His wonderful love in thinking of me,
And dying to save me on Calvary's tree.

The Lord is my portion,—earth's portion is vain,
'Tis burdened with sorrow, and sickness, and pain;
Oh! gladly I'll leave it on hearing His call,
Then prostrate before Him in gratitude fall.

HYMN OF PRAISE.

THOU God that rulest earth and Heaven,
To Thee be praise and glory given;
Let all on earth behold Thy power
And goodness in each passing hour.

How shall we praise Thy matchless love
In Thy Son's mission from above?
Who came to raise a fallen race,
And fit them for a nobler place.

Oh, touch us all with holy fire,
Our breasts with gratitude inspire;
That we may teach all those who stray,
The narrow, sure, and only way.

Oh, keep us in the narrow road,
Until in Heaven we meet our God;
Then shall we endless praises sing,
And Heaven with "hallelujahs" ring!

THE HOUSE OF GOD.

HENCE ! every thought of worldly care,
  This is the House of God ;
My soul, as for a feast prepare,
  Thy burdens here unload.

The pealing organ sweetly rings
  Its cadence everywhere ;
From pew to pew bright angel-wings
  Seem floating through the air !

Ah ! God is here—how very near—
  We speak to Him in prayer ;
His voice so dear dispels our fear,
  And soothes our every care.

From out His Holy Word we read
  His promises secure ;
" Yea and Amen " they are indeed,
  And ever shall endure.

The man of God, with solemn voice,
  Expounds " the message " given ;
And as he speaks our hearts rejoice
  As if approaching Heaven.

He dwells upon the love of God,
  So boundless, pure, and free ;
And of His Son, who bore the rod,
  And died upon the tree.

The rich and poor, the young and old,
  Here like one family meet,—
One heavenly shepherd and one fold,
  And one communion sweet.

Dear day! the best of all the seven,
  My heart with rapture swells;
'Tis as the melody of Heaven,
  The sound of Sabbath bells!

Like doves unto their downy nest,
  Our souls fly out to thee:
Sweet foretaste of that heavenly rest
  For souls from sin set free.

THE CHRISTIAN'S ARMOUR.

Ephesians vi., 10—18.

OH! Christian brother! would'st thou know
    From whence thy strength should be,
When wrestling with thy bitter foe,
    Who seeks to conquer thee?

With might from God, the Lord, be strong,
    And in His strength prevail;
With heavenly armour battle wrong,
    And thou shalt never fail.

Thy loins be girt about with truth,
    The truth of God is sure;
'Twill compass all the snares of youth,
    And keep thee ever pure.

Let righteousness thy breastplate be,
    To ward thee in the fight;
Love God and man—deep, strong, and free,
    By morning, noon, and night.

Shod with the preparation
    Of holy Gospel peace,
The footsteps of the godly man
    From strength to strength increase.

The shield of faith, above all, see
    That it be clear and bright;
From it the fiery darts shall flee,
    And vanish from thy sight.

Salvation's helmet guards thy head,
  And shields from hurt thy face;
Inscribed upon it may be read:
  "A SINNER SAVED BY GRACE."

Thy right hand grasps the two-edged sword,
  With firmness and with might;
The true-dividing of God's Word
  Is justice, truth, and right.

Then polish up thy armour bright,
  With vigilance and care,
And thou shalt conquer in the fight,
  By patience, faith, and prayer.

Let prayer like incense ever rise
  To God from souls set free;
Until we gain the heavenly prize,
  And His own image see!

THE LORD'S PRAYER,

(PARAPHRASED).

1. *" Our Father, which art in Heaven."*
    FATHER of Lights and God of Love,
    Thrice Holy is Thy name;
    Thou King of Kings, enthron'd above,
    Thou ever art the same.

2. *" Hallowed be Thy name."*
    Forever hallowed be Thy name
    By hosts in earth and Heaven;
    In heathen lands make known Thy fame,
    And saving mercy given.

3. *" Thy Kingdom come."*
    Thy kingdoms stretch from pole to pole,
    Throughout earth's utmost bound;
    Till gathered in each blood-bought soul,
    That on the earth is found.

4. *" Thy will be done on earth as it is in
        Heaven."*
    Thy will be ours from morn till night,
    Obedient to Thy Word;
    Then shall our path be clear and bright,
    And sin shall be abhorr'd.

5. *" Give us this day our daily bread."*
    That man shall nothing be denied,
    Who truly seeks Thy face;
    Our earthly wants are all supplied
    With bounty, love, and grace.

6. "*And forgive us our trespasses.*"

> Our sins and failures we confess,
>   On bended knee entreat ;
> Thus, trusting to Thy tenderness,
>   We'll worship at Thy feet.

7. "*As we forgive them that trespass
>   against us.*"

> And may Thy love our hearts incline,
>   To mercy bend our ear ;
> To pardon others who combine
>   To cause us hurt or fear.

8. "*And lead us not into temptation,
>   but deliver us from evil* "

> From Satan's tempting snares of sin,
>   Thy right hand shall deliver ;
> Our God shall keep us pure within,
>   Though Hell's foundations quiver.

9. ' *For Thine is the Kingdom, the power,
>   and the glory, for ever.*"

> Thine are the kingdoms of the earth,
>   And thine the glory ever ;
> This world did own Thee at her birth,
>   Thou everlasting Giver.

10. "*Amen !* "

> Amen ! Amen ! so let it be,
>   God's counsel faileth never ;
> The Truth of God is pure and free,
>   And shall prevail for ever !

C

THE LONGING SOUL.

OH! blessed Jesus, cast on me
    One look of pitying love;
That moment shall my soul be free,
    And sing with saints above.

Thy all-sufficient love is such
    That none need ever fear,
Or think that they can ask too much,
    Nor doubt Thy presence near.

In life or death, in weal or woe,
    In sunshine, shade, or shower,
To Thee in pray'r my thoughts shall go,
    And bless each passing hour.

Then, Saviour, teach me what Thou wilt,
    Oh, save me from my sin;
Cleanse Thou my soul from all its guilt,
    And make me pure within.

Then shall I walk with God on earth,
    And dwell with saints in Heav'n;
Thus sanctify this second birth
    By saving mercy giv'n.

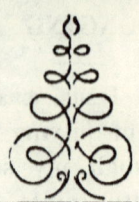

SONNETS.

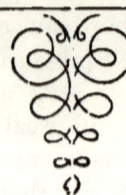

Sonnets.

THE LAST ENEMY — DEATH.

DEATH comes to all, no man can stay his hand ;
If he but calls, the proudest in the land
His summons must obey, and then be led
By his cold, icy hand 'mong silent dead ;
There to remain till Death himself shall die,
And He who conquered Death shall reign on high.
Oh, Death ! where is thy sting if Jesus save ?
Where, then, thy victory, O cruel grave ?
Thou hast no power o'er him whom God defends,
For him all things subserve most glorious ends.
Death but relieves from earthly pain and woe,
A friend, though in the guise of mortal foe.
Oh, may the grave to me be but a door
To that bright land where Death shall reign no more !

THE MASTER'S CALL.

GO work to-day! the fields are white to view,
The harvest truly great, the labour'rs few;
To you the call is giv'n, reapers, obey!
Work mightily, while yet 'tis called to-day!
The night approacheth when no man can work,
And sin and vice do in the darkness lurk.
The fields are many and the world is wide,
O'er trackless forests, deserts, stormy tide,
Proclaim that love which makes all mankind kin,
And saves the soul though steep'd in direst sin;
Which frees the captive, gladdens the opprest,
And leads the erring to the Saviour's breast;
Where pard'ning mercy, love, and joy are giv'n
To make this earth a sweet foretaste of Heaven.

THE SABBATH SCHOOL TEACHER'S
REWARD.

OH, teacher, faint not ! thou art not alone,
He who hath called thee will thy labour own ;
And though, at first, no grateful fruit appear,
Think not 'tis labour lost, but persevere ;
Yield not the conflict to the Master's foe,
But still " from strength to strength " unwearied go.
Plant thou the seeds of heav'nly truth with care,
And water oft with fervent, pleading prayer,
Then leave the rest to God, whose Spirit's pow'r
Shall cause the seed to grow, the plant to flow'r,
Till in due course the ripen'd fruit appears
To cheer thy heart, reward thy prayers and tears,
And make thee sing for joy,—that peace bestow
Which they who serve the Lord alone doth know.

A PRAYER FOR WISDOM.

1 Kings iii., 11, 12; Prov. iii., 13—18.

OH ! let me ever walk in Wisdom's way,
That I may wiser grow, and day by day
Prove that her paths are pleasantness and peace ;
And, therein walking, may my years increase
In fruitful days of labour and reward,
Of love, and joy, and peace, and sweet concord.
Grant me the work which angels most enjoy,—
A life well spent in Heaven's blest employ,
In deeds of love, and works of holy zeal,
And in that occupation may I feel
The kind approval of a God of grace,
Who owns His servants with a smiling face ;   .
My work accepted, and my sins forgiv'n,
Bless'd while on earth, and doubly bless'd in Heaven.

JESUS, MY REFUGE.

"A hiding place from the wind and a covert from the tempest; as the shadow of a great rock in a weary land." —ISA. xxxii. 2.

OH, grateful shelter from the storms of life,
From cares corroding or from worldly strife;
Fain would my panting soul Thy shadow seek,
And, shielded safe, in grateful accents speak
Of all Thy love to man, whose strength Thou art,
Whose refuge sure, the uplifter of the heart
Of him who strives to seek Thy safe retreat,
And loves with Thee to dwell—there at Thy feet
Lay sorrow's burden down; Thy gracious gift
Accepts with thankful heart, nor seeks to lift
With sinful hands once more the heavy load
That bars the soul's communion with his God;
Oh! there would I in calm repose abide,
Safe as THE ROCK near which I seek to hide.

CHRISTIAN, AWAKE !

CHRISTIAN, awake ! thy life is not a dream,
You cannot glide for ever with the stream ;
'Tis like the ocean in her changing moods
Of great uproar, or calm, deep solitudes ;
Her varying tides a ceaseless motion keep,
And danger ever haunts the mighty deep ;
Yet o'er her bosom in majestic pride
The noble vessel doth in safety ride,
Defying all the stormy winds that blow,—
Making a highway of a raging foe,
Till the bright haven doth appear in view,
Which speaks of rest to all the weary crew ;
Where, sails all furl'd, anchor firm and fast,
They rest the sweeter for the dangers past !

THE NAME OF JESUS.

SWEET name! what cadence in the very sound!
What heav'nly music in the utt'rance found,
When whisper'd in the ear of dying saint,
Tho' spent with pain, and pulse and heart beat faint;
Yet, at the name of " JESUS " doth his eyes
Seek ours in love, and peace, and glad surprise,
And then forever close in sweet content
To open them in Heav'n—a life well spent!
Oh, Jesus! Thine the ever-potent power
To charm, to heal, to bless, in trial's hour;
Let all the world Thy name with rev'rence hear,
And trust Thy pow'r to save; with holy fear
Approach the footstool of Thy matchless grace,
And find in Thee their soul's dear resting-place!

THE SABBATH-DAY.

SWEET day of rest ! most precious of the seven,
God's gracious gift to man, in mercy giv'n
That he may cease from toil and worldly care,
And for that brighter rest his soul prepare.
Blest harbinger of that eternal day,
Whose beams shall never fade or pass away.
Oh, may we ever watch with jealous eye,
And careful guard the hours that swiftly fly,
That nought but heav'nly themes our thoughts
    engage,
And with temptation hourly warfare wage ;
Oft by " the footsteps of the flock " be found,
Within the house of God, on praying ground,
And there our grateful hearts shall homage pay,
To Him who rose triumphant on that day.

THE IMAGE OF THE HEAVENLY.

ALMIGHTY God ! in all Thy works display'd,
For man in Thine own image Thou hast made ;
How should we, then, Thine every law respect,
And mourn in dust and ashes if neglect
Of ours should once but mar that Image bright,
And, grieving Thee, turn sunshine into night.
Let not our hearts from Thee be turn'd aside,
But let Thy Holy Spirit with us 'bide ;
Then shall our life be like the flowers in June,
Displaying sweetness, and our hearts in tune
To the pure melodies of heav'nly song,
Which to the ransom'd hosts of Heav'n belong ;
Thus here below let glorious anthems rise
To mingle with the songs of Paradise.

THE PEACE OF GOD.

THERE is a peace the world can not bestow
Nor take away ; and they in joy do go
Who but possess it, for its charm is sure,
And doth through all the ills of life endure ;
It makes the soul rejoice, the weak feel strong,
The troubled soul burst forth in joyous song,
Which may be heard above the din of strife,—
An antidote for all the cares of life !
Oh ! peace of God ! may I thy pow'r enjoy,
Then in thy praise my life shall find employ ;
Thou shalt me 'fend from every evil way,
Make all my darkness turn to brightest day,
Till, safe within the everlasting arms,
My soul shall rest secure from all alarms !

CONSCIENCE.

CONSCIENCE is the true monitor of God
For our approval, or a very rod
Of direst chastisement for evil deeds,
Or wicked thoughts that grow like noxious weeds
Within the garden of the human heart,
To mar the buds and flowers which would impart
A fragrant solace to the weary soul
Of God-made man, thus strengthen and control
His better nature in Temptation's day,
And drive the hateful thoughts of sin away,
To hide themselves for very shame of sin,
And, hence renewed, the better life begin :
Thus, Conscience, listen'd to, will safely guide
Where perfect peace and happiness abide !

SEEKING AFTER KNOWLEDGE.

WISDOM is the true currency of Heaven.
From fools withheld, but to the prudent giv'n;
In her pursuit let us in earnest be.
If we would prosper, therefore, let us see
That all our energies be so combin'd
As best to cultivate the heart and mind.
This occupation is the best that can
Engage the youth, or occupy the man
In leisure hours, which, be they rightly spent,
Are of great moment, and by Heaven lent
To sweeten toil, and relaxation give
To dull and cank'ring cares, which, while we live,
Must be our lot; our time, then, let us spend
As best becomes us, knowing not our end!

THE DRUNKARD'S FATE.

FOR the drunkard there's no such place as "home,"
Though over the face of the earth he roam,
Till Death shall unfetter the drink-bound slave,
And he findeth " rest " in the silent grave;
His untimely death—" the wages of sin,"—
Satan's reward for the worship of Gin !
He gave up his wife and his children dear
For the drink which he thought his heart could cheer ;
But the more he drank the lower he sank,
From the highest grade to the lowest rank,
Till for shame, his name a bye-word became,
And he lost for ever his once fair name :—
For the pleasure of drink, which he loved so well,
He barter'd his soul to the lowest hell !

TEARS.

TEARS are the outflow of great joy or grief,
    The speechless language of a swelling heart,
Whose fitful solace is a sure relief
    For joys excessive, or affliction's smart;
The valve-escapement of a pent-up soul,
    Whose fulness finds expression in a tear ;
Which, like healing balm, makes the wounded whole ;
    Or dearest friend—when darkest hour is near—
Whose hands we clasp in friendship's sacred hold,
    And cling to them like ivy round the tree,—
Weakness and strength combined in love's enfold,—
    Then let the flood-gates open full and free !
Our bitter tears but give us strength to bear
Affliction sore, or joy's too sudden glare !

REST!

REST is the peaceful calm which follows toil:
    Sweet to the labouring man who tills the soil;
Likewise most precious to the weary brain,
Tired with the dull routine of loss or gain;
Or to the authors of our learned books,
Who show the trace of study in their looks—
All value rest—all need those quiet hours
As much as doth the plant those welcome show'rs
Which Heaven sends to cool the fevered earth,
And cause glad Nature sing aloud with mirth.
When God at first created earth and skies,
He "rested" in the shades of Paradise!
Likewise shall we, earth's care and labour o'er,
Find rest the sweeter for the toils we bore!

PAIN!

WE shrink and recoil at the touch of Pain,
Yet know that escape from his grasp is vain;
And our trembling hearts with emotion swell
As we sigh and groan at each painful spell;
But the dreadful hour of suffering past,
And our courage and health restor'd at last,
How soon we forget our terror and pain,
And mingle once more with the world again;
But not as before, for a tender string
Hath been set to music, and thus deth sing:
I have suffered, and feel for others' pain
A twinge of my own past sorrow again!
Ah! Pain, what a useful teacher thou art,
Lessons of sympathy thus to impart!

WHAT IS LOVE?

LOVE is the grateful off'ring of a heart
In all its fulness to some counterpart,—
Zeal answering zeal, each striving to excel,
Zealous to share the glowing thoughts that dwell
In hearts united by Love's silken bands,
Each thread some joy Love only understands.
'Mid stirring echoes of a fond desire
Claim kindred feelings and a sister-fire,
Joining life's hopes in one ecstatic song,
As sweetest music from an angel-throng;
No doubt or fear disturbs Love's peaceful rest,
Nor cares corroding rankle in her breast;
Each thought bears fruit in others sweeter still,
Till earth seems heav'n, and heav'n seems own'd at
    will.

TORONTO.

FAIR Toronto! Queen City of the West!
Of all thy sister-cities thou art best:
As far as eye can reach, from Don to Humber,
Are chimneys, tow'rs, and spires in goodly number, —
Cathedrals, churches, schools, and mansions rise,
In stately grandeur tow'ring to the skies.
A noble harbour fronts thy southern bound,
And gentle hills encircle thee around;
From North to South, and East to West expand
Streets, Avenues, and Roads, so wisely plann'd
That strangers visit thee with ease, and find
In thee a home at once just to their mind:
Long live Toronto! loud her praises swell,
Here Commerce, Art, and Nature love to dwell!

TORONTO.

Long live Toronto! loud her praises swell,
Here Commerce, Art and Nature love to dwell
PAGE 54.

TORONTO BAY.

Toronto Bay! by morning, noon, or night,
Thy waters charm me with some now delight!
PAGE 57.

TORONTO BAY.

OH, lovely scene of ever-changing hue!
Dark ocean-green, or sky-bright azure-blue;
Swift o'er thy heaving bosom gaily float,
The trim-built yacht, gay skiff, or pleasure-boat;
Or, here and there, a light birch-bark canoe
Lends a romance to the enchanting view.
Toronto Island, in the distance, seems
The happy fairy-land of boyhood's dreams,
Where naught but Pleasure dwells, and music fills
The balmy air with melody that thrills
Each bounding heart with ecstasy and joy,
And happiness the fleeting hours employ!
Toronto Bay, by morning, noon, or night,
Thy waters charm me with some new delight!

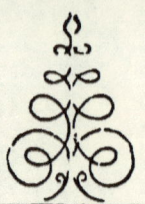

PATRIOTIC.

Patriotic.

FAIR CANADA.

LAND with the inland seas,
Swept by the mighty breeze,
 Fair Canada;
Here many nations dwell,
Loving their freedom well,
Reaping where forests fell,
 Fair Canada!

Land of the prairies wide,
Stretching like ocean's tide,
 Fair Canada;
Land of green hill and dale,
Mountain and pleasant vale,
Here worth shall never fail,
 Fair Canada!

Fair as an opening flower,
Planted in Heaven's bower,
 Fair Canada;
Reaching from sea to sea,
Great will thy future be,
Land of the brave and free,
 Fair Canada!

Come, then, from many lands,
Brave hearts and willing hands,
    To Canada ;
Come where rich virgin soil
Waits to reward your toil,
Share in the harvest spoil
    Of Canada !*

---

* This " Canadian National Song." may be sung to the
air of " The National Anthem," the 1st verse of which
would be very appropriate as " a finale " to the above
composition.

CANADIAN SONG OF FREEDOM

FREEDOM'S glad song we sing:
Free as a bird on wing,
Free as the sweet pure air,
Free as the sunlight fair.

Shout Freedom's holy song:
" We nothing fear but wrong;
For Freedom, God, and Right,
We'll nobly stand and fight !"

While life and strength remain
We will our rights maintain;
Our hardy sons of toil
Shall guard Canadian soil.

We shed no craven tear,
No tyrant's threat we fear;
Before no foe we fly,
We dare be free—OR DIE !

To death we only bend,—
Our foe, and yet our friend;
The watchword of the free
Is :—" DEATH OR LIBERTY ! "

WELCOME HOME, BRAVE VOLUNTEERS!

Song of Welcome, sung by the School Children at the City Hall, Toronto, in honour of the Volunteers' return from the North-West Rebellion, 1885.

WELCOME home, brave Volunteers !
    Welcome, welcome home !
Gone are all our anxious fears,
Answer'd now our pray'rs and tears,
Welcome home 'midst ringing cheers,
    Welcome, welcome home !

Welcome to our loving arms,
    Welcome to your rest ;
Welcome home from war's alarms,
Safe from death and all that harms,
Victory hath crown'd your arms,
    Welcome to your rest.

Canada is proud of you—
    Soldiers brave and true !
Ye have dar'd to win or die,
Ye have made the rebels fly,
Let your standards wave on high,
    Soldiers brave and true !

Welcome home, though wounded sore,
 Battling for the right;
Dreadful marches now are o'er,
Safe from deadly bullets' pour,
Silent now the cannons' roar,
 Heroes from the fight!

Welcome home, but some we miss,
 Brave hearts, where are they?
Gone where noble spirits are,
Gone beyond the reach of war,
Sleeping peacefully afar,
 'Neath the sod and clay.

Welcome home, our soldiers dear
 Welcome, welcome home!
Rebel threats no more we hear,
War's alarms no more we fear,
Now we smile and dry the tear,
 As we welcome home!

NIAGARA FALLS.

OH, Niagara! as at thy brink I stand,
    My soul is filled with wonder and delight,
To trace in thee that wonder-working Hand,
    Whose hollow holds the seas in balance light!

Worthy art thou to be a nation's pride,—
    A patriot's boast—a world's unceasing wonder;
Like some bold monarch calling to thy side
    Subjects from every clime in tones of thunder!

Deep on my soul thy grandeur is impress'd,
    Thy awful majesty—thy mighty power;
Thy ceaseless tumult and thy great unrest,
    Like nations warring in dread conflict's hour!

Rainbows of glory sparkle round thy shrine,
    Cresting thy waters with effulgence bright;
And in thy foaming currents intertwine
    Rare corruscations of commingl'd light!

Like roar of battle, or like thunder's call,
    Thy deep-toned echoes roll with solemn sound;
Like pillar'd clouds thy vapours rise, and fall
    Like sparkling pearls upon the thirsty ground!

Rush on ! rush on ! in thy uncheck'd career,
  With avalanchic power thy course pursue ;
While rending rocks quake as with mortal fear,
  And stand in awe to let thy torrents through !

Naught but the hand of God could stay thy course,
  Or drive thee back to Erie's peaceful keep :
Then onward press with thy gigantic force,
  Till in Ontario's bosom lull'd to sleep !

Emblem of Freedom ! who would dare essay
  To bar thy noisy progress to the sea ?
Then onward press ! while bord'ring nations pray
  For strength and wisdom to be great and free !

THE DOMINION OF CANADA.

AN HISTORICAL SKETCH.

" ONLY a few acres of snow ! "
　　Our country first was styl'd,
By French explorers long ago,
　　In winter bleak and wild.

An hundred years roll'd on apace,
　　Again they sought our shore,
As summer beam'd with smiling face,
　　Inviting to explore.

The noble Champlain and his band
　　On Quebec's height did raise
The flag of France, with eager hand,
　　'Mid thankful prayer and praise.

They fought and toil'd for many years,
　　And till'd the virgin soil,
Till happy homes dispell'd their fears,
　　And fortune sweeten'd toil.

Grim War again chang'd peaceful scenes
　　To carnage and dismay ;
But British prowess intervenes,
　　And finally holds sway.

Then hand-in-hand, a peaceful band,
  The Briton and the Gaul
Agree'd to sub-divide the land,
  Together stand or fall !

May peace and honour ever keep
  The brothers thus entwined ;
With patriotism—pure and deep—
  Fidelity enshrined !

At last, like fair unfolding flow'r,
  The New Dominion stands,—
Upper and Lower Canada
  Embrace with loving hands !

Thus July first of every year,
  Our great Dominion Day,
Her loyal sons hold ever dear,
  In honour and display !

The fairest flower on this fair earth,
  The freest of the free ;
Whose sons are proud to own their birth,
  And claim their homes in thee !

CANADA'S DEFENDERS.

Written on the occasion of the return of our brave Volunteers from the North-West Expedition, 1885.

HOME again our Volunteers,
Home again 'mid ringing cheers,
Vanishing our anxious fears,
    Canada's defenders ;
From the scenes of strife and war,
From the rifle-pits afar,
True as steel or Polar star,
    Canada's defenders.

Back to home and kindred dear,
Back to lov'd ones waiting here,
Back from death and every fear,
    Welcome, brave defenders ;
Ye did make a noble stand,
Under Middleton's command,
For the honour of our land,
    Welcome, brave defenders.

Welcome back to peace and joy,
Welcome back to your employ,
Rebel threats no more annoy,
    Canada's defenders ;
Stretching wide from sea to sea,
Canada may boast of thee,
Soldiers daring, brave, and free,
    Canada's defenders.

Let us join the merry throng,
Welcoming with shout and song,
Singing praises loud and long,
 To our brave defenders ;
Ye have made the rebel Riel,
Cower 'neath your charge of steel,
Own your pluck, and then appeal
 To our brave defenders !

QUEEN VICTORIA'S JUBILEE.*

Music by Prof. J. F. Johnstone.

Our no - ble Queen, all hail! On this thy Ju - bi - lee;

True hearts shall never fail To love and hon - our thee.

Vic - to - ri - a, to thee, From loy - al hearts and free,

At this glad time, from ev'-ry clime, Come shouts of Ju-bi - lee.

Vic - to - ri - a, to thee, From loy - al hearts and free,

At this glad time, from ev' - ry clime, Come shouts of Ju-bi-lee.

* Lines in honour of the 49th anniversary of Her Majesty's accession to the Throne of England, June 20th, 1837: thus 1886—87 may be termed "Queen Victoria's Jubilee," and all loyal subjects will rejoice with her on whose Dominions, it is said, " *The sun never sets!*"

QUEEN VICTORIA'S JUBILEE!

OUR noble Queen, all hail!
  On this thy Jubilee;
True hearts shall never fail
  To love and honour thee.

> CHORUS.—Victoria, to thee!
>   From loyal hearts and free,
>   At this glad time,
>   From every clime,
>   Come shouts of Jubilee!

From every land on earth
  Thy sons send greetings full,
And proudly own their birth
  Beneath thy sovereign rule.—CHORUS.

In many scenes of life
  Our hearts round thee entwine;
As mother, Queen, or wife,
  Thy virtues nobly shine.—CHORUS.

Let rebels point with scorn,
  Or cowards quake with fear,
Thy true sons—British-born,
  In memory hold thee dear.—CHORUS.

God spare thee many years,
  In trouble send relief;
At last a nation's tears
  Shall wet thy grave in grief!—CHORUS.

QUEENSTON HEIGHTS.

A VERBAL PICTURE.

OH! that I had the artist's power to touch
 The speaking canvas with a master-hand,
I'd paint a scene I truly love as much
    As any landscape in this fair new land!

That picture would be Queenston's lovely height,
    'Neath which Niagara's rushing waters gleam,
Like molten glory in the sunset bright,
    Or fancy's vision in a pleasant dream!

Here two great nations meet as if to kiss,
    Divided only by a silver line;
Peace, welfare, harmony, and mutual bliss
    Link fruitful branches of a parent vine!

The setting sun would tint Niagara Town
    With gilded glory as he sinks to rest;
A noble steamer bearing swiftly down
    Toward Ontario's heaving, billowy breast!

The stately monument of Brock would stand
    In bold relief against the azure sky,—
The valiant leader of a noble band
    Who for their country's honour dar'd to die!

A picture thus I'd paint in Nature's praise,
    And worship at the threshold of her door;
Before the scene I stand in rapt amaze—
    In silence dumb—yet love it all the more!

QUEENSTON HEIGHTS.

Here two great nations meet as if to kiss,
  Divided only by a silver line;
Peace, welfare, harmony, and mutual bliss
  Link fruitful branches of a parent vine!

Page 76.

ODE TO LAKE ONTARIO.

THOU inland sister-sea, Ontario!
   To glide upon thy bosom is sublime;
There note thy peaceful, steady, onward flow,
   Ceaseless and constant as the course of time!

Thy waters seem the same,—yet ever new—
   Fed by a thousand streams on either side;
The same clear sky, the same thy depths of blue,
   Free as the nations bord'ring on thy tide!

Vast upper-lakes feed thee with lib'ral hand,
   From higher lands as new as thine hath been;
Where still the Indian and his wigwam stand,
   He half amaz'd with what his eyes hath seen!

To thy embrace—like gallant lover bold—
   Niagara rushes in his mad career,
Till tir'd and spent, past whirling eddies cold,
   He calmly sinks to rest when thou art near!

Last of the inland seas!—yet nearest home—
   Thy waters soon shall swell the mighty deep,
And mingle with the ocean's briny foam,
   There shalt thou rest—and there for ever sleep!

SONS OF SCOTLAND.

Respectfully dedicated to Robert Burns Camp, No. 1,
Sons of Scotland, Toronto.

SONS of Scotland! land of freedom!
　Sons of noble sires, all hail!
Let your watchword aye be " Freedom !"
　　You shall evermore prevail !
Let the wrong be deeply hated,
　Let the right be prized like love,
Martyr-courage unabated,
　　Trusting in your God above!

Sons of Scotland! bards historic
　Sang your deeds of noble fame,
Let not tyranny plethoric
　Tarnish your unsullied name ;
History gives us what we cherish,
　Ours to still maintain the right,
May that history never perish,
　　Though we perish in the fight!

Like the waters from our fountains,
　Giving strength to flesh and bone ;
Like the thistle on our mountains,
　Harmless, if but let alone !
Ours to shield the needy stranger,
　Ours to put the erring right ;
Ours to stand in time of danger,
　And, if need be, ours to fight !

Dear old Scotia! land of flowers,
  Land of mountain, hill, and vale ;
Land of sunshine, shade, and showers,
  Land of river, loch, and dale ;
Land of ever-changing beauty,
  Land of liberty and love ;—
Scotchmen ! tread the path of duty,
  Till you reach the land above !

THE THISTLE.

"NOW, why do Scotchmen use the Thistle
      As emblem of their country dear;
A useless plant, with many a bristle,
      One scarce can touch without a fear!

"There must be some good cause, I gather,
      Why such a flow'r should be their pride;"
I ask'd the question of my father,
      But he my ignorance did chide!

"My boy, let history truly tell,
      Of by-gone years of war and strife,
When noble sires fought long and well,
      And for their country gave their life!

"O'er flood and field, o'er brake and fen,
      The fierce invader sought our land;
Out-number'd were our gallant men,
      But, ah! they made a noble stand!

"One morn, before the break of day,
　　Our foes crept near our slumb'ring camp;
They might by stealth have won the day,
　　Did not one on a Thistle stamp!

"A cry of pain our sentries heard,
　　A quick alarm then was given,
At once each gleaming sword was bar'd,
　　And backward Scotland's foes were driven!

"Since then the Thistle is our pride,
　　'*Gae, touch me if ye daur,*' it says;
And Scotchmen true, where'er they 'bide,
　　Revere the Thistle all their days!"

TO GLASGOW, SCOTLAND.

DEAR Glasca! aft I think o' thee,
    An' happy days lang syne,
Though distant, thcu art dear tae me,
    By memory's sacred shrine;
Aft hae I climb'd Balmano's steep,
    An' ran doon Portlan' brae,
An' gather'd "gushes" in a heap,
    Wi' mony a gled "hurra!"

In summer time, whan schule was out,
    An' we had got "the play!"
I've wannert mony a mile about
    The hale lang simmer's day;
A favourite place was Glasca Green,
    By bonnie banks o' Clyde,
Where Nelson's monument is seen,—
    Our hero an' our pride!

An' aft we went by Broomielaw,
    Tae Renfrew's cosy toon,
There mony a noisy luckless craw
    We manag'd tae shoot doon!
Then ower the Clyde, tae Kelvinside,
    We took oor hameward way,
Weel pleased tae ride tae whaur we'd bide,
    Sae tir'd were we that day!

Oh! Glasca, dear! I've drapt a tear
  O' happiness an' joy,
At a' thy memories sac dear
  Whan I was bit a boy!
Three thoosan' miles are stretch'd atween,
  My new hame an' my auld,
Yet in my heart sweet memories green,
  S'all bide till I'm deed cauld!

THE DYING SCOT ABROAD.

"AH, me! ah, me!
    An' maun I dee,
Sae far frae kith an' kin?
    How prood I'd be,
    If spar'd tae see
The lan' ma heart bides in!

"I've wannert far,
    In peace an' war,
An' fought for Scotlan's Queen,
    Yet here I dee,
    Sae far frae thee,—
Saut tears fill up my e'en.

"Dear freens an' kind,
    Please bear in mind,
An' send this message hame:
    My mither dear
    Wad like tae hear—
I trust in Jesus' name."

'Mid friends' sad sighs
    He clos'd his eyes,
And pass'd from earth to Heav'n;
    Yet, e'en in death,
    With latest breath,
His thoughts to "HOME" were giv'n.

THE DYING SCOT ABROAD.

―――

"Ah, me! ah, me!
An' maun I dee,
Sae far frae kith an' kin;
How prood I'd be,
If spared tae see,
The lan' my heart bides in."

PAGE 86.

LOVE, HOME, AND FRIENDSHIP.

Love, Home and Friendship.

WHERE DOTH BEAUTY DWELL?

LOOK for the first faint streaks of morn
  That gilds the eastern sky,
Another day in beauty born,
  As mounts the sun on high;
Tinting the tops of highest towers
  With crimson and with gold,
Melting the dew-drops from the flowers
  That peepingly unfold:
There doth "the beautiful" abide
  In calm security;
The rosy morn—deck'd like a bride—
  Of virgin purity!

Look for the eyes that beam with love,
  And sparkle with delight,
To meet thy gaze—like stars above—
  Brightest in thy dark night;
Dispelling every thought of sin
  From out thy heart's great deep;
Chasing the darkness from within,
  Or soothe thy fears to sleep:
There doth "the beautiful" abide
  In full maturity;
And there may thy fond heart reside
  Through all futurity!

HEART QUESTIONINGS.

WHAT stirs an emotion
        As deep as the ocean,
And strong as the hills that tower above?
        'Tis the sound of a sigh,
        As the zephyrs go by,
That tells in a breath the presence of Love!

        What is seen in the glance,
        As true lovers advance,
That kindles a flame which never can die?
        'Tis a spark from above,
        From the altar of Love,
Dropp'd unerringly down from on high!

        As the loving hands clasp,
        What is told in the grasp
That quickens the pulse and glows on the cheek?
        'Tis "the story of old,"
        In that loving enfold,
The language of Love that words cannot speak!

        Whence the tones that can thrill,
        Without effort or will,
And woo the heart's fond admiration?
        They are notes from the choir,
        With the golden lyre,
Tuned by Love's sublime inspiration!

Oh! from whence comes the bliss
Of love's first fervent kiss,
That rapturous outflow of feeling?
'Tis a faint echo given
Of earth's foretaste of Heaven,
By fond hearts their fulness revealing!

Whence the breathings of soul
That defies our control,
Those sweet communings of heart with heart?
'Tis a gift from above,
'Tis the token of love,
Once possesss'd, time or death cannot part!

THE STAR OF LOVE.

IS Love a star?
Yes, 'tis a star
Of heav'nly magnitude afar;
In darkest night
The purest light,
No baneful doubt should ever mar.

It is a star—
The Polar star—
That guides the sailor on the sea,
Where'er he roam,
To love and home,
Across the boundless ocean free.

Storms may arise
In life's pure skies,
And gathering clouds bedim our day;
But Love's bright eye,
Like star in sky,
Will seek to guide us on our way!

Love reigns supreme,
An endless theme,
Love rules the world with gentle hand;
As captives, we
Desire to be
Encircl'd with her golden band!

TRUE LOVE

'TIS a magic spell,
    Which lovers know well,
In sunshine and shower the same;
    Ever old, yet new,
    Both constant and true,
And seeks neither self nor fame.

    Unheard or confest,
    As seemeth it best,
Its tale it may never unfold;
    Yet all know the pow'r
    Of Love's happy hour,
Its memory never grows old!

    'Tis a golden key,
    Be it sigh or plea,
That opens the door of the heart:
    And treasures untold
    Doth ever unfold,
Which riches could never impart.

Then cherish with care
A jewel so rare,
And dim not its lustre with scorn;
'Twill lighten the gloom
From cradle to tomb,
And heal the heart bleeding and torn.

Love never can die,
Its home is on high,
And God will yet claim what He gives;
And love He hath giv'n,
To make earth a heav'n,
True love in the heart ever lives!

THE HUMBER "FAIRY."

HEARD ye of the Humber "Fairy"?
Know ye that her name is Mary?
Queen of beauty—light, and airy,
    Winsome, yet so shy;
In a cottage by the river,
Where the green ferns nod and quiver,
There my fancy turneth ever,
    For her smile I sigh!

When the sun is slowly setting,
Then, my heart with fulness fretting,
All but love of her forgetting,
    To my skiff I hie;
Off to "my Fairy-land" I glide,
Each feather'd oar on either side
Like Cupid's wings, they skim the tide—
    O'er the waters fly!

O'er the Bay the moon is stealing,
All her loveliness revealing,
Then to each fond heart appealing,
    Love looks eye to eye!
Glide we up the Humber river,
Where the rushes sigh and quiver,
Plight our love to each for ever,—
    Love that will not die!

A SOUVENIR OF LOVE.

Tenderly.   (Copyrighted.)   Music by E. Gledhill.

Dearest, sweetest, fondest, best, Lean your head   up-on my breast;

Lov-ing arms shall thee entwine, Loving hands   be plac'd in   mine;

Throbbing hearts with pleasure beat, Happy   eyes   in gladness meet;

Peace and   joy now reign supreme, Love our all   absorbing theme....

Dearest, sweetest, fondest, best, Lean your head   up-on my   breast;

Lov-ing arms shall thee en-twine, Loving hands   be plac'd in   mine.

A SOUVENIR OF LOVE.

DEAREST, sweetest, fondest, best,
Lean your head upon my breast;
Loving arms shall thee entwine,
Loving hands be placed in mine;
Throbbing hearts with pleasure beat,
Happy eyes in gladness meet;
Peace and joy now reign supreme,
Love our all-absorbing theme.

Picture of a living love,
True as angel-notes above;
Constant as the Polar star
Shining in the heavens afar;
Deep and boundless as the sea,
Ever pure and ever free;
Warm and bright as Scuthern skies,
Earthly Eden—Paradise!

Love like this doth ever sing,
Echoes wake and echoes ring;
Love and pain *may* sometimes meet,
Love can make the pain a sweet;
Grief and care shall flee away,
Darkest night be turn'd to day,
Winter snows to Summer showers,
Autumn leaves to Spring's fresh flowers.

Sordid pleasures have their day,
Truth and Love shall ne'er decay;
Heaven and earth their blessings give,
Love and Truth shall ever live.
Then, let Love our bosoms thrill,
Empty hearts may have their fill;
The poorest may be rich in love,
Bless'd on earth and crown'd above!

EYES THAT SPEAK.

GIVE me the eyes that speak of Love,
  And sparkle in their gladness,
Like twinkling orbs of light above,
  Dispelling care and sadness;
Which make this earth a Paradise,
  Though humble be our dwelling,
And causing thoughts of love to rise
  From hearts with fulness welling.

Give me the eyes whose tears of Grief
  Are shed for our condoling,
Whose sympathy is sure relief
  To hearts that need consoling;
More precious than the jewel rare
  That glistens in its setting,
Are eyes that speak the love they bear,
  All selfishness forgetting.

Give me the eyes that speak of Peace
  And shed a halo o'er us,
Whose beams can cause all strife to cease,
  And tune our hearts in chorus
To sing in unison the strain
  Which God hath set before us:
"Let peace on earth for ever reign,"—
  Hark! angels join the chorus!

Give me the eyes of Faith to see,
    Behind the clouds of sorrow,
My Father's hand still guiding me
    On to the bright to-morrow;
And onward still, through good and ill,
    His eye shall safely guide me;
All dangers past, safe home at last,
    With Jesus close beside me!

WHAT CAN LOVE DO?

LOVE can make the eyes shine bright,
Love can brighten darkest night;
Love can make the lover gush,
Love can make the maiden blush.

Love can warm the coldest heart,
Love can kindest words impart;
Love can happiness bestow,
Love can never answer " No. "

Love can sing the gayest song,
Love can make the weak feel strong;
Love can lighten every care,
Love can sweetly trials bear.

Love can sit enthron'd in state,
Love can rule a nation great;
Love can noble laws impart,
Love can win the people's heart.

Love can educate the mind,
Love can aye be true and kind;
Love can greatest pleasure give,
Love can teach us how to live.

Love can sweetest comfort bring,
Love can take from Death the sting ;
Love can greatest burdens bear,
Love can all our sorrows share.

If our lives are pure and free,
Love must then our teacher be ;
Daily learn the heavenly plan :—
" Love to God and love to man."

LOVE'S PROGRESS.

WE met, but not as strangers meet,
In busy mart, or crowded street,—
No hurried glance could well suffice
To meet the gaze of Love's surprise;
That look a "tale of old" reveal'd,
Which would not, could not, be conceal'd,
And well bespoke Love's sweet content,
Though speechless on our way we went.

Again we met—not like the past,—
The spell of Love had now been cast;
Still, words refused to tell the tale
Which redden'd cheeks that erst were pale,
And fluttered hearts with new-born joy,
And gave our thoughts such sweet employ;
We smiled, and often met to smile,
And thus did Love our hearts beguile.

At last I spoke, in hope and fear,
A few short words, deep, true, sincere;
Then love in transport met the gaze
Of love return'd 'mid glad amaze;
Her stammering tones, and modest start,
Answered the gladness in my heart;
I kissed joy's tear from off her face,
And clasp'd her in my warm embrace.

G

We loved, and love still dwells secure,
And shall while life and love endure ;
Our love is sweet, and all is well,
For in each other's hearts we dwell ;
Like streams which meet and onward glide,
Till lost in ocean's boundless tide,
We two have met no more to part,
For Love hath join'd us heart to heart !

LOVE-LINKS.

THE LOOK of a loving eye
   Tells all it knows,
   Like blushing rose,
And lives to be lov'd—or die!

The TOUCH of a gentle hand
      A tale doth tell
      Love knoweth well
And only Love understand.

The TONES of a loving voice,
      Like birds in Spring,
      Doth sweetly sing,
And maketh the heart rejoice!

The JOY of a love-lit heart
      No tongue can tell:
      Its potent spell
Neither time nor distance part!

Sweet words that can never die;
   "Wilt thou be mine?"
   "I WILL BE THINE!"
Is the maiden's faint reply.

These LINKS must not be broken,
      Oh! no! no! no!
      But stronger grow,
Love's changeless, deathless token!

HOME.

THE sweetest word on earth is HOME,
　　To loving hearts most dear ;
Where'er our footsteps seek to roam,
　　Home thoughts are ever near.
The memories sweet of life's spring-day
　　Keep fresh and green for ever,
Like fragrant flowers they scent the way
　　Adown life's winding river.

Our homes may be where mountains rise
　　Like dark-green clouds to Heaven ;
Or where the valley-lily lies
　　Our humble lot be given ;
Or on an island of the sea
　　Oft by the tempest prest :
No matter where our homes may be,
　　To each that home is blest.

The strongest love within man's breast
　　Is love of life and home,
Like fledglings hovering round their nest
　　Our thoughts encircle home ;
Our years may reach three-score and ten,
　　And full of changes be,
Yet scenes of home will haunt us then
　　When life was pure and free.

Where love hath cast her golden spell
  And kindest deeds are done,
Where loving hearts unite to dwell
  'Tis heaven on earth begun ;
Then cherish home with jealous care
  And let not strife prevail :
Thus for our " heavenly home " prepare,
  Secure within the vail.

THE FLOWER OF THE FAMILY.

THE Angel of Death came hovering near,
    To kiss the fair cheek of a child ;
He left a dark shadow of hope and fear,
    And a mother's heart throbbing wild.
A fond father knelt, with a trembling heart,
    By the couch where his treasure lay ;
Though he tried to smile, yet the tears would start,
    While he vainly brush'd them away.

The silence of death was broken at last,
    By sobs of a mother's first grief,
As the eyes of her boy to hers were cast,
    With appealing looks for relief ;
The father's strong arms encircl'd the child,
    And sooth'd him at last to his rest,
While he clos'd his eyes and lovingly smil'd,
    As he winged his way to the blest !

A prayer for submission and faith was sent
    To the God of all love and grace ;
And a ray of light in the dark was lent
    From their heavenly Father's face,
As He taught them to lift their hearts above
    The flower which to them was given ;
While He would transplant, with infinite love,
    That flower in the garden of Heaven !

ROMPING WITH THE CHILDREN.

MIMIC battle,
　　Din and rattle,
Romping with the children after tea;
　　How they giggle,
　　Laugh and wriggle,
Crowing as they triumph over me!

　　"Make him a horse,"
　　That's "Pa," of course,
They, the merry riders full of glee;
　　Though not much ground,
　　Yet round and round,
Till they drive the wind right out of me!

　　At last content,
　　And I near spent,
Loudly they call for "a song" from me!
　　I laugh and grin,
　　And then begin,
Hugging a little one on each knee!

Some song they know,
Sung soft and low,
Soon makes them feel like sleep, do you see?
Then, one by one,
To bed they run,
With "a good-night kiss" for Ma and me!

God bless their rest,
Our lov'd and best,
May their lives be ever pure and free;
Their joys we share,
And banish care.
While we laugh and romp so merrily!

"OUR JOHNNIE."*

WE hae had a happy time,
　　Since hame cam Johnnie ;
Wi' a face like angel sweet,
Stealin' a' o'or kisses neat,
Creepin' roun on hauns an' feet,
　　Was o'or wee Johnnie !

Langest day maun hae its close,
　　Alas ! puir Johnnie ;
Death cam in sae grim an' cauld,
Chill'd the lammie in the fauld,
Ta'en the young and left the auld,
　　Puir deed wee Johnnie.

Ta'en awa' in life's spring-time,
　　O'or ain dear Johnnie ;
Mither's heart in anguish wild,
Faither grudges sair his child,
Yet tae God baith reconcil'd ;
　　We'll gang tae Johnnie.

---

* Lines written on seeing the above epitaph on a tomb-
stone over a little grave in Mount Pleasant Cemetery,
Toronto, erected in affectionate remembrance of John
McKinnon, born Oct. 7, 1874; died Jan. 31, 1881.

Ainst the licht o' a' o'or house,
        O'or ain wee Johnnie;
Noo the licht is ta'en awa'
Darkness seems tae cover a',
Nane can comfort us ava
        Bit o'or wee Johnnie!

'Neath the souchan willow tree
        Lies o'or wee Johnnie;
Just beneath a hillock green,
Whaur the daisies may be seen,
Wi' the buttercups between,
        Sleeps o'or wee Johnnie.

Aft we shed the bitter tear
        For o'or wee Johnnie;
Then look up wi' faith abuin,
Whaur nae sorrow creepeth in,
There, secure frae death an' sin,
        Bides o'or wee Johnnie!

"PAPA'S PET."

DOWN a crowded thoroughfare
    Walk'd a little stranger,
Light blue eyes and golden hair,
    Scarcely knew her danger!

Gaily dress'd, so clean and neat,
    Ribbons without measure!
Stockings white and slipper'd feet,
    Some one's darling treasure!

Heedless pass'd the crowd along,—
    Business hours are pressing,
None in all that busy throng
    Stopp'd to make caressing!

Now and then an anxious look
    O'er her face came stealing,
Wise as any sage's book,
    Troubled heart revealing!

Looking for her mother's smile
    In that sea of faces;
None her fears could there beguile,
    Wearily she paces!

See! the blue eyes fill with tears,
    And her bosom, heaving,
Shows the crowd her anxious fears
    Need some kind relieving!

Soon a kindly stranger came,
    And wip'd the cheeks so wet :—
"Tell me, Sissy, what's your name?"
    "My papa calls me ' *Pet!* '"

Here the stranger dropt a sigh,—
    A sigh of sad regret ;
One he claim'd above the sky,
    Ah ! once he call'd her " *Pet!* "

How he kiss'd that little child,
    Kiss'd all her tears away ;
Till at last she sweetly smil'd,
    Just like a summer's day !

Soon he found her father's home,
    Kept chatting all the way ;
Never more from thence to roam
    Until her wedding day !

LEARNING "THE TWINS" TO WALK.

TWO little "Toddlekins" learning to walk,
    Mamma and sister supporting;
Trying to toddle, and learning to talk,
    'Mid chatting, laughing, and sporting!

Mamma seems proud of her two little pets,
    Johnnie and Winnie she calls them;
Dolly consumes all the kisses she gets,—
    No "Dolly" could thrive without them!

One little—two little—three little steps!
    Cautiously, carefully tended;
Mamma's strong arms most lovingly "keps"
    Both when "the trial" is ended!

Laughing, and crowing, and kissing all 'round,
    Everyone happy and cheerful;
A hug and a squeeze, a skip and a bound,
    A din that's perfectly fearful!

Happy the home with the children around,
    Despite all their din and rattle;
No likelier spot on earth can be found
    To nerve us for life's stern battle!

A KISS THROUGH THE TELEPHONE.

Copyrighted.   Music by H. F. Sefton.

The Tel - e - phone, in mer - ry tone, Rang

"Tink - el - ty - tink - el - ty - tink!" I

put my ear Close up to hear, And

what did I hear do you think? I

put my ear Close up to hear, And

what did I hear, do you think?

A KISS THROUGH THE TELEPHONE.

THE telephone,
   In merry tone,
Rang " Tinkelty-tinkelty-tink !"
   I put my ear
   Close up to hear,
And what did I hear, do you think ?

   " Papa, hello!
      'Tis me you know!"
The voice of my own little Miss ;
   " You went away
      From home to-day,
But you never gave me—a kiss!

   "It was a mistake,
      I was not awake,
Before you went out of the house ;
   I think that a kiss
      Will not be amiss
If I give it—sly as a mouse !

"So here goes, Papa,
And one from Mamma,
And another when you can come home ;
Just answer me this,
Is it nice to kiss
When you want through the dear telefome ?"

"Hello?" I replied,
With fatherly pride,
"I've got them as snug as can be ;
I'll give them all back,
With many a smack,
As soon as I come home to tea!"

A KISS THROUGH THE TELEPHONE.

"Papa, hello!
'Tis me, you know!"
The voice of my own little Miss;
"You went away
From home to-day,
But you never gave me—a kiss!"

THE BABY'S PORTRAIT.

STEADY now, young " Chatterbox! "
Rosy cheeks and raven locks;
Mamma wants your portrait now,
Smile again and smooth your brow!
Touch your mouth with finger-tips,
Pearly teeth and ruby lips;
Papa's pride and mamma's pet,
High upon a cushion set!

Rolling eyes of azure blue,
Watching, wondering, "what's-a-do!"
While the artist smiles and grins,
Ere he to his task begins.
Steady now, young " Chatterbox! "
Sly as any little fox;—
Tinkling bells—the signal given—
"One, two, three, four, five, six, seven!"

For a minute silence reigns,
Pleasure leaps in all our veins,
Baby's picture 's now complete,
Lifelike, true, and oh, so sweet!
Every one is positive
Never was such negative;
Beauty smiles at beauty's self,
Each one hugs the little elf!

H

Soon a dainty frame is made,
In the frame the portrait laid,
Where it lay for many a day,
As the years roll'd swift away ;
Oft the mother look'd and smil'd
At the picture of her child,
Now a happy, blushing bride,
Still her father's joy and pride !

But at last there came a day
When the bride must pass away,
Claim'd by lover of her own,
Happy in that love alone ;
And, 'mong presents rich and rare,
One was prized—a portrait fair--
Smiling as in days of yore,
Now a " Chatterbox " no more !

"COME, LET US LIVE FOR OUR CHILDREN."—*Frœbel.*

GATHERING wildflowers in the wood,
  Joyous and free as the air ;
Happy days of early childhood,
  Touch'd not by sorrow or care.

Break not the spell of their gladness,
  Let not the sorrow creep in ;
Shield them from trouble and sadness,
  Soon will earth's worries begin.

Listen to story and prattle,
  Join in their joy and their glee ;
Scold not their din and their rattle,
  Make them to feel they are free.

For other years will come apace,
  Brimfull of care and toil as ours ;
When they will fill our vacant place,
  And bless the memory of these hours.

"OUR BABY!"

CHUBBY face,
Full of grace,
Comic little glances;
    Glad surprise,
    Roguish eyes,
Making sweet advances!

    Rosy feet,
    Small and neat,
With dainty little toes;
    Snug and warm,
    Safe from harm,
Done up in fancy hose!

    Gaily drest,
    In her best,
Just like a fairy queen;
    Tiny hands,
    Satin bands,
We're proud of her, I ween!

Kick and crow,
Stretch and grow,
Seems bigger every day;
Not a care
Nestles there,
But angel-smiles alway!

God above,
Full of love,
Sent this little stranger;
Now we pray,
Every day,
Shield her from all danger!

THE MOTHERLESS CHILD.

" OH! Papa, where is Ma to-day?
   I've looked in every bed!
They tell me 'Ma has gone away,'
   Aunt says that ' Ma is dead.'
I thought that she would soon be well,
   I kiss'd her yesterday;
Now where she is I cannot tell,
   I feel too sad to play."

The father, stooping, kiss'd his child,
   And strok'd her golden hair;
He strove to hide the anguish wild
   That struggl'd with despair.
The blue eyes scann'd him o'er and o'er,
   And seem'd to read him through:
" Papa, will Mamma come no more,
   And has she left you too?"

Like arrow sharp from quivering bow,
   The question smote him sore
And grief, like ocean's ebb and flow,
   Found vent in tears once more.
He clasp'd his darling to his breast,
   Which seemed to ease his pain:
" God called your Ma; His will is best;
   We'll meet with her again!"

He carried her with tender care
  To where the coffin lay,
To view the mother, young and fair,
  Now lifeless as the clay.
Oh! Mamma, dear! I'm here! I'm here!
  My Papa is here too!"
And on the dead there dropt a tear
  From out those eyes of blue!

Kind friends looked in and view'd a scene
  Which "touched their hearts," they said,
Then tenderly they came between
  The living and the dead.
Weep not for those whom God has ta'en
  To realms of endless light,
Our loss is their eternal gain—
  God doeth all things right.

A GOLDEN WEDDING.

FIFTY years of wedded life,
  Half a century of bliss,
Since we first were man and wife,
  What a consummation this !

Through the sunshine and the shower,
  Bound by golden bands in one,
Hand-in-hand in darkest hour,
  We the race of life have run.

True to vows of early years,
  Faithful to each other's love,
Yet with tenderness and tears,
  Ripening for the courts above.

Years of joy, and love, and peace,
  Full of happiness and trust ;
Learning, as the years increase,
  God is ever wise and just.

Soon at last His voice will call
  One or other hence away ;
Still remaining ONE through all,
  WEDDED THROUGH ETERNITY !

TO MY FRIENDS.

FRIENDS of my early days and years,
Ye who dispell'd my infant fears,
And o'er me spent your prayers and tears,
　　　　Father, Mother;
And let me pay a tribute meet
To those who watch'd my infant feet,
And shower'd on me their kisses sweet,
　　　　Sister, Brother.

Friends of my school-days or of play,
When all was joyous, bright, and gay,
Companions dear of life's spring-day.
　　　　Again we meet;
As memory paints the scenes anew,
In colours of the brightest hue,
When life was good, and pure, and true,
　　　　And friendship sweet.

Friends of those years when hopes were high,
And hearts beat true, and love was nigh,
And echoes woke which ne'er shall die,
　　　　But echoes give;
While fleeting years roll on apace,
Within my heart there is a place
That bears the likeness of each face,
　　　　And thoughts that live!

Friends dead and gone—friends far and near—
Friends tried and true—friends ever dear,
Though sunder'd far, yet all are here,
　　　Close to my heart ;
And all along life's rugged way
The smile of friendship crowns the day,
And hearts are young though heads be grey :—
　　　Friends never part !

A TRIBUTE TO MOTHER.

OH, mother, dear! what memories sweet
  Call back the scenes of early years,
When thou didst tend our infant feet,
  And guard our life with pray'rs and tears.

Our little griefs, at school or play,
  We pour'd into thy willing ear;
But thou didst kiss the tears away,
  And quick dispell'd our every fear.

And, when in wilful ways we trod,
  Alas! for us, too willing feet,
Thy love did bring us back to God,
  And led us to the mercy-seat.

Thy look was love—thy smile was joy—
  Thy tears the eloquence of grief;
Thy loving voice found sweet employ
  In whisp'ring to our heart's relief.

Oh! mother dear! how much we owe
  To thee, for all thy loving care;
While memory lasts our thoughts shall go
  Back to the days of love and pray'r.

Though on this earth no more we meet,
  And surging seas between us roll,
We yet shall meet at Jesus' feet,
  Where love eternal fills the soul!

BEREAVED.

I miss a dear face
From its wonted place,
And my heart is full of sadness;
But looking above
To the God of love,
The sorrow is chang'd to gladness.

For I know that there,
In that purer air—
The home of our heavenly Father—
Is the one I miss,
In that land of bliss,
Where the angels love to gather.

And a voice that cheers,
Through the silent years,
Is heard with its sweet, soft pleading;
And a hand that guides
Through earth's stormy tides
Hath mine in its kindly leading.

I must not repine,
But daily incline
The path of my lov'd one to follow;
Then let the years pass,
Like sands in a glass,
Or sighing winds over the hollow.

Oh! we yet shall meet
On that golden street,
And never again shall we sever;
Earth's troubles all past,
In our home at last,
With fulness of joy for ever!

A HUSBAND'S BIRTHDAY GREETING.

DARLING, awake! and let the sweet, glad light,
Fill eyes that love hath made so pure and bright;
So calm and deeply true, so free from guile,
So winning in their artless love-lit smile,
That I would fain obey their least behest,
And clasp thee fondly to my throbbing breast,
And tell, with untold kisses, sweetest dear,
That thou hast entered on another year!

How sweet the memory of the blissful past,
When o'er our paths love's glad spring-flowers were
        cast,
As fresh and pure as when in Eden's bowers
The first fond pair spent earth's creative hours;
Yet, dear, 'twas but the dawn of brighter days,
Such as we now enjoy, 'mid grateful praise
To Him who crowns our years with peace and love,
A sweet fore-taste of purer joys above!

Ah! clinging dear! the ivy and the oak
Are not more near when thou dost thus provoke
To deeds and words of love that plainly tell
That Love is king, and all he doth is well;
The hot tears flow, but not because of grief,
'Tis heartfelt joy which thus must find relief;
And mutely eloquent each throbbing heart
Proclaims the other as its counterpart!

God bless our love, for He alone can bind
In perfect union, both of heart and mind,
All those who seek in Him their source of bliss,
Of love and joy, of peace and happiness.
Oh, may thy future bright and joyful be,
From every sorrow may thy lot be free,
And through life's journey to the very end
Heaven's choicest blessings all thy way attend !

A WIFE'S LAST GOOD-BYE.

OH, husband dear, though now we part,
   And I must cross the river,
I fain would cheer thy lonely heart—
   We do not part for ever !
I go to brighter, holier ground,
   Where friendships are not hollow,
Where peace and love are ever found,
   And thou wilt surely follow.

Oh, brightly beams that happy land
   Of light, and love, and gladness,
Where we shall stand, at God's right hand,
   Free from all care and sadness.
Let faith foresee with hopeful eyes,
   That even now may borrow
A cheering ray from brighter skies
   To dissipate thy sorrow.

Oh, husband dearest, fondest, best,
   To whom my love was given,
In Jesus' love find sweetest rest,
   We'll wait for thee in Heaven ;
Death cannot enter there, my love,
   Nor tears bedim the sight ;
An endless love is ours above,
   With angels ever bright.

One child is safe with me in Heaven,
   The other left with you,
May wisdom from above be given
   To make him kind and true;
And when at last we four shall meet,
   Beyond the surging river,
We'll lay our crowns at Jesus' feet,
   And praise His love for ever!

A BOUQUET OF FLOWERS.

THE present you send,
My dear loving friend—
A beautiful bouquet of flowers,—
    Is precious to me,
    As coming from thee,
With perfume of bright sunny bowers.

    It reminds me of home,
    Where once we did roam,
'Mid flow'rs in the garden at play;
    As swift pass'd the hours
    In Flora's sweet bowers,
And short seem'd the summer's long day.

    But life, like the flowers,
    Hath changeable hours,
And sunshine and show'r intervene;
    Yet love in the heart
    Can beauty impart,
And help to make life " evergreen."

    Let friendship and truth
    Encompass our youth,
From sorrow and trouble 'twill save;
    In sweetest content
    Our lives shall be spent,
And flow'rs strew our path to the grave!

TO A LITTLE FRIEND.

AN ACROSTIC.

Jesus was once a little child,
Obedient, loving, lowly, mild;
His mother's pride, His father's joy,
No evil did His heart employ.

Alexander, may that spirit
  Which was in Him be found in you;
And His blessing duly merit,
  By being ever kind and true.

Carefully guard the days of youth,
On every hand temptation scorn;
Refresh thy mind with heav'nly truth—
Many are thus to glory borne.
In all thy ways acknowledge God,
E'en when beneath His chast'ning rod.

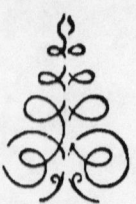

MISCELLANEOUS POEMS.

Miscellaneous Poems.

A SUMMER'S DAY;

OR,

MORNING, NOON, AND NIGHT.

INTRODUCTION.

SPRING show'rs have wash'd the winter snows
      away,
And Nature smiles at the approach of May,
Clad in the brightest green, and deck'd with flowers,
Which speak of balmy winds and sunny hours;
When birds, and bees, and butterflies abound,
And flowers in rich profusion deck the ground,
Strewn here and there by Flora's wanton hand,
And Hope sings merrily o'er all the land:
    Oh! then, 'tis surely summer!

I.—MORNING.

'TIS morning! for the rising sun
  His daily journey hath begun;
Flooding the earth with glory bright,
Chasing away the gloom of night;

Closing the eye of every star
That twinkles in the heavens afar ;
Paling the moon's soft, silvery light,
Till it recedes from mortal sight !

All hail ! thou ruler of the day,
Nature delights to own thy sway ;
At thy approach the smallest flower
On hill, or dale, or, verdant bower,
Lifts up its head, though wet with dew,
And spreads its petals out to view,
To cheer the heart, and glad the eyes,
A dainty morning sacrifice !

At Sol's glad light the feather'd throng
Make woods resound with cheerful song,
And, full of grateful, glad surprise,
Fly out to meet thee in the skies ;
The milkmaid sings a merry lay,
As through the fields of fragrant hay
She gaily trips to meet the cows,
Whose welcome noise the echoes rouse.

Sweet morning hours !—first-fruit of day—
None but the slothful spurn away
Thy gifts of beauty, health, and light,
And, slumb'ring, turn thee into night !
When glory gilds the eastern sky,
And Nature lifts her voice on high,
Why should not man, with grateful heart,
Join in and take a noble part ?

II.—NOON.

——

THE sun hath reached meridian's height,
And robed the earth in glory bright;
Flora, arrayed in all her charms,
Looks up and smiles; with loving arms
Seeks to invite his presence near,
Like perfect love which hath no fear,
And thinks no evil, though now a show'r
Should hide his face in noontide's hour!

Bright noon! when all around is life,
And hum, and stir, and busy strife;
Nature, in all her various forms—
Like angry waves in wintry storms—
Strives life with life for daily bread,
For all must live and all be fed,
Each eager to secure a prey
Before noontide shall pass away!

The butterfly enjoys the hour,
And sips sweet nectar from the flower;
The humble bee doth homeward bring
Her treasures sweet on laden wing;
The cheerful sparrow on the ground
A dainty mid-day meal hath found,—
All nature knows the time of day,
Nor lets it idly pass away!

'Tis noon ! and from the village school
A joyous host, released from rule,
Rush out with hearts as light as air,
Without a sorrow or a care,
But to improve the fleeting hour
Whether in sunshine or in shower,
For noon's short hour flies fast away
When given to joyous mirth and play !

III.—NIGHT.

THE evening shades are falling fast,
Long shadows on the ground are cast,
The western sky is all aglow
With fiery glory setting low ;
The hill-tops glance with changing hue,
A noble back-ground to the view,
As mountain, river, lake, and plain,
Are bathed in glory once again !

Sweet evening hours ! suggesting rest,
To weary toilers thou art blest ;
See yonder cottage at whose door
The children look for " Pa " once more,
And by the welcome they impart
Bid all the cares of day depart ;
Domestic joys are life's sweet flowers,
Full blooming in the evening hours ;

As evening deepens into night,
A host of stars shed purest light;
Fair Luna comes upon the scene,
With halo of bright, silv'ry sheen,
To woo the lover out to stroll
The shady walks with love-lit soul,
And pour into the maiden ear
The soulful words she loves to hear!

At last the midnight hour is past,
The stillness of the grave is cast
On all around with potent spell,—
The day is past and all is well!
For Israel's God doth ever keep
His watchful eye o'er those who sleep;
Tired Nature rests, while God alone
With heavenly love protects His own!

NATURE'S TEMPLE.

'TIS sweet to sit in pensive mood,
  'Mid Nature's grand, stern solitude.
Where warbling birds pour forth their lays,
In happy, joyous songs of praise.

Or watch some noble cat'ract bound
From giddy height to lowly ground,
Where echoes ring from peak to peak,
And God in Nature seems to speak.

With praise to God the woods resound,
Surrounding hills repeat the sound,
And in my heart an echo rings,
Which joy and consolation brings.

There doth my soul find sweet relief,
And gather strength for future grief;
For life's stern duties here prepare,
By supplicating God in prayer.

Oh, God! to be alone with Thee,
In Nature's Temple—rich and free;
And for a time forget the strife
Of man with man—of Death with Life.

Oh, happy hour! oh, sweet retreat!
With Thee, my Father, thus to meet;
And learn from Nature to adore
The God of Nature evermore!

NATURE'S TEMPLE

Or watch some noble cataract bound
From giddy height to lowly ground,
Where echoes ring from peak to peak,
And God in Nature seems to speak.

A CHRISTMAS CAROL.

RING out the merry Christmas bell
   That tells of joy and gladness,
Our happy hearts with pleasure swell,
  This is no time for sadness ;
This is the crowning of the year,
  A day of merry-making,
With feast and song our hearts we'll cheer,
  All anxious cares forsaking.

'Twas Christmas-tide when Jesus lay
  All lowly in a manger,
He came to take our sins away,
  And save our souls from danger ;
The shepherds on the hills at dawn
  Heard angel-voices singing :
"Now peace on earth, goodwill to men,
  We are this morning bringing."

'Tis eighteen hundred years and more
  Since that glad Christmas morning,
Yet once a year, on every shore,
  Are happy hearts adorning
The Christmas tree with presents rare,
  Its dark-green boughs are laden,
And round it dance the children fair,
  The lover and the maiden!

Oh ! merry, happy Christmas Day,
　For young and old together,
The very snow-flakes seem more gay,
　Though bitter cold the weather;
As round the family fireside
　Our dear ones we are meeting,
Let peace and harmony abide,
　With love each other greeting.

FAITH ILLUSTRATED.

THE night was calm and still, the moon shone
        bright,
And lent the silver-sweetness of her light
To guide the lonely patrol on his beat,
As, with a measured step, from street to street,
His echoing footsteps beat a solemn tread ;
And from the city towers, far over head,
The midnight hour rang out with mournful chime,
Telling the wakeful of the march of time.

But hark ! what awful sound is that I hear,
Which falls like thunder on my closing ear ?—
Fire ! *fire !* FIRE ! 'tis the patrol's warning cry
That rings from house to house, from earth to sky,
Rousing the wakeful, scattering the dreams
Of love and joy, and for a moment gleams
From face to face—from eye to eye—
A terror as of death or danger nigh.

Fire ! *fire !* FIRE ! onward press the anxious crowd,
With rushing, hasty steps, and noises loud,
To yonder mansion, where the ruddy glare
Speaks louder than the groans of dark despair !
The greedy flames surround with furious power
The doomed abode ; and in that midnight hour
Strong men are weak, and none but they are brave
Who look to Him whose power alone can save.

Thus felt a father when he saw his child,
Far out of human reach, 'mid danger wild,
On top-most storey, and in blank despair,
His piteous cries resounding through the air.
At last he heard his father's well-known voice,
Which made his sinking heart with hope rejoice,—
"Spring to my arms, my son ! do not delay,
Haste ! haste ! and I shall bear thee safe away !"

The brave child heard and, stepping on the sill,
Prepared to execute his father's will ;
He looked from death to life with anxious eyes,
And ceased his murmur and despairing cries.
Then, with his tiny arms outstretched to Heaven,
Heroic courage to his soul was given ;
He. fearless, sprang from all the dread alarms,
And fainting, dropped into his father's arms.

O let such FAITH be mine,—such childlike faith
In Thee, O God ; then neither fear nor scathe
Shall hinder me from clinging to Thine arm,
For Thou alone canst save from fear or harm !
And when, at last, *Thy call* from earth I hear,
No doubt shall hinder, nor despairing fear ;
But, looking up to Thee with heart and eyes,
Thou wilt accept and bear me to the skies !

A BIRTHDAY GREETING.

TIME is ever on the wing,
   Fast our moments fly away;
Let us prize them, though they bring
   Joy and sorrow mixed alway!
Had we joy alone, my friend,
   We would seek no other sphere;
Did God only sorrow send,
   We would wish the end was near!

God is wiser far than we,
   And He knoweth what is best;
Let us in His wisdom see
   That He seeks our FAITH to test!
May we live, as though this hour
   Were our last on earth to spend;
And, come sunshine, shade, or show'r,
   God's best blessing will attend!

Let the years roll on apace,
   Heaven is nearer than before;
Let us bravely trials face,
   Waves break loudest near the shore!
Summer, Autumn, Winter, Spring,
   All within one year are bound;
Let us through each season sing
   Songs of praise the whole year round!

K

FLOWERS!

FLOWERS are lov'd by young and old,
As they gracefully unfold
Sweetness caught from Eden's bowers,
When at first God made the flowers:
Rich in every tint and hue,
Smiling through their tears of dew;
Beauty's glory crowns their head,
As they peep from grassy bed!

Purity the Lily seems,
As she in the sunlight gleams;
Humility the Pansy knows,
Happiness bespeaks the Rose;
Love, the laughing Daffodil,
Pinks our eyes with *Beauty* fill;
Every flower, a charm its own,
Fills a place on Flora's throne!

Flowers may teach the heart of man,
As no other teacher can:
God's creative hand was there,
When He made the flowers so fair;

Out of chaos formed the earth,
Spake, and planets had their birth ;
To adorn the human race,
Lent the beauty of His face !

He who loves the tiny flower
Something knows of Heaven's power,
Which will hope and courage give,
Strength and sweetness while he live ;
Like the flowers we pass away,
Short, yet sweet, is life's brief day—
Let good deeds and thoughts sublime,
Stand the touch and test of time !

TO THE PANSY.

OH, Pansy! with the velvet hue,
And spots of gold, and pearly dew;
How gracefully you hang your head,
Scarce rais'd above your humble bed.

I love you for your queenly grace,
Your happy smile, your winsome face;
In sweet retreats you love to dwell,
And lend the vale thy beauty-spell.

Sweet emblem of a "heart at ease," *
Thy form my inmost fancies please;
In quiet beauty you excel
All other flowers in wood or dell.

Thou mightest well be Flora's queen,
If thou wouldst let thy charms be seen;
And seek to vie with other flowers
That deck with beauty kingly bowers.

But thou art wise to grace the spot
Where God has cast thy humble lot;
And there, secure from rude alarms,
Display thy modest, winsome charms!

When I look up from thee to God,
And see His glory in the sod,
My heart in sweet tranquility
Would learn from thee "HUMILITY!"

* This flower is sometimes called "Heart's-ease."

LIFE'S PROGRESS

Rivers rolling to the sea
 Loose themselves in ocean,
Bearing on their bosom's free
 Noble ships in motion

   *   *   *   *   *   *   *   *

Ah! soon we'll reach life's ocean strand,
 Just like the winding river
Safe in the hollow of that Hand
 Which holds the seas for ever.

PAGE 103.

LIFE'S PROGRESS.

DOWN the mountains, down the hills,
  Trickling on for ever;
Gentle springs make little rills,
  Little rills the river.

Rivers rolling to the sea
  Lose themselves in ocean,
Bearing on their bosoms free
  Noble ships in motion.

Such is life, a constant change,
  Still from small to greater;
Let us learn the lesson strange
  Taught by our Creator:

Life is giv'n for noble ends,
  Lofty thoughts and actions,
Winning to our bosom—friends
  Gain'd in life's transactions.

Ah! soon we'll reach life's ocean strand,
  Just like the mighty river,
Safe in the hollow of that Hand
  Which holds the seas for ever.

TWO POOR ORPHAN BOYS.

GOD help poor orphans, for they need
Our Father's watchful care indeed;
Out in the cold wide world alone,
Where strangers speak with freezing tone;
With none to take them to their heart,
Or dry the burning tears that start
From sunken eyes and hollow cheek,
Which want, neglect, and hunger speak.

Two years ago their father died,
And soon their mother, by his side
In one cold grave was laid at rest,
And join'd the everlasting blest;
The greatest pain she felt at death
Was whisper'd with her dying breath:
" God keep my boys when I am gone,
Poor, helpless orphans, all alone ! "

Ah ! how they struggl'd for their bread,
And oft went supperless to bed ;
And, sometimes, neither bed nor board
Their scanty pittance could afford.
Oft in the storm, and snow, and sleet,
They travell'd on with cold, wet feet,
And sought that kindly passers-by
Would pity the poor orphans' cry !

Sometimes a crossing neatly swept,
By one at either end, was kept,
Where, now and then, an honest cent
Was earned by them with great content.
As long as work is brisk they feel
No evil tempting them to steal,
Or beg, or whine, or seem dismay'd,
Or of their lot feel half afraid.

Dear Christian people, help such boys,
Who little know of earthly joys:
Do speak to them with kindly tone,
And make the orphan's cause your own;
Try if your purse can spare a cent—
Or e'en a dime—to God 'tis lent,
And make their sad and painful lot
By kindness almost half forgot!

LAUGHING.

OH, how I love the hearty laugh
   That rings with a merry peal!
The outcome of some witty "chaff,"
   Which makes one cheerful feel;
A laugh which almost racks the jaw,
   A regular side-splitter!
In which all join with "loud guffaw,"
   And nothing in't that's bitter!

I love when children laugh outright,
   And shout in their playful glee,
When all run out to see the sight,
   Or join in the sport so free!
A laugh that knows not care or ill,
   The frolicsome laugh of fun!
Which speaks of naught but right good-will,
   As they skip, and laugh, and run!

I hate the haughty laugh of scorn,
   From the dudish fops called "*men*,"
Who sneer at worth if humbly born,
   And smile at "the upper ten!"
Whose empty laugh shows lack of brain
   Their language devoid of wit,
Their greatest feat to "twirl a cane,"
   Or display "*a perfect fit!*"

A LESSON FROM THE CLOCK.

TICK, tick, tick, tick,
Time flies so quick,
With never ceaseless motion;
Our moments pass
Like sands in glass,
Or wavelets of the ocean.

Thus moments go,
For weal or woe,
And none returneth ever;
How mindful we
Should ever be
To spend with wise endeavour.

The life of man
Is but a span,
Short, transient, and fleeting;
With here and there
A joy or care,
A parting or a meeting.

Then let each hour,
Like beauteous flower,
Some fragrance send to Heaven;
To God above,
In grateful love,
Let ransomed powers be given.

THE POWER OF SONG.

HE poet's heart is ever young,
His thoughts are light and gay ;
To Nature's praise his harp is strung
In sweetest harmony.

The minstrel's soul is all aflame
With passion's holy fire ;
He courts the Muse in love's sweet name,
And kindles with desire.

He joins the children in their play,
And pleases them with song ;
He soothes them off to sleep alway,
With lullabies of song.

His heart is touch'd with others' woe
In deepest sympathy :
His tears with theirs together flow
In tuneful symphony.

For tyrant-threats he hath no fear,
But wages bitter strife
With all that dares to interfere
With liberty and life.

The soldier on the tented fiel
Feels that his cause is strong,
For Freedom's enemy must yield
Before the Patriot's song.

THE POWER OF SONG.

The power of song to stir the soul,
  Or soothe the human heart,
Is felt by man from pole to pole,
  Or distant isles apart.

Like notes from Heaven's angelic choir,
  Or herald-angel's song,
Our minstrels with poetic fire
  The echoes still prolong!

PAGE 168.

The sailor on the stormy sea
  Beguiles the hour with song,
As, whistling for the winds so free,
  He steers his bark along.

The reapers by the waving corn
  Doth make the welkin ring,
And when the harvest home is borne
  The harvest-song they sing.

The power of song to stir the soul,
  Or soothe the human heart,
Is felt by man from pole to pole,
  Or distant isles apart.

Like notes from Heaven's angelic choir,
  Or herald-angel's song,
Our minstrels, with poetic fire,
  The echoes still prolong!

THE LITTLE NEWSPAPER BOYS.

TWO little brothers left their home
    One cold, bleak winter's day,
All round the city streets to roam,
    But not in childish play.

They on a noble errand went,
    An honest dime to gain,
By selling papers—well content
    To brave the sleet and rain.

One ten year's old was brother " Bill,"
    And six year's old was " Jack ; "
They trudged along with right good-will,
    Though business was quite slack !

Yet bravely shouts the elder boy :
    " My papers! who will buy ? "
And at each sale a smile of joy
    Lights up each cheerful eye.

The weary hours of night wore past,
    The steeple clock struck Nine :
One bun between them eased their fast,
    But Jack began to pine.

" Oh ! Bill, I'm tired and sleepy now,
    I'll sit down here and rest ; "
And soon the cold and chilly brow
    Dropp'd feebly on his breast.

His brother Bill, with courage high,
 More energy display'd,
"The latest news!" did loudly cry,
 Not daunted or afraid.

Yet, now and then, dear little Jack
 Would look with tearful eye
On brother Bill, as he came back
 To tell him—"not to cry!

"I've nearly sold them all now, Jack,
 There's only three to sell;
When they are sold, high on my back
 I'll ride you home pell-mell!"

At last their merchandise was gone,
 Ten cents was fairly won!
And Bill knelt down to help Jack on
 His back, for the home-run!

Dear Christian people, help such boys
 To earn an honest cent,
They little know of earthly joys,
 And yet seem well content!

TO THE FOUR WINDS OF HEAVEN.

OH ! cold NORTH WIND from the Polar seas,
  Thy breath congeals lake, brook, and river ;
You strip the leaves from the tallest trees,
  And make them bend, and sigh, and quiver !

Oh ! blow, SOUTH WIND from the coral strand,
  Thy breath is sweet with the flowers' perfume ;
Thrice welcome thou to our cold North land,
  To cheer our hearts with the rose's bloom !

Oh ! blow, EAST WIND, with thy favouring gales,
  To speed our ships from the mother-lands ;
And glad our eyes with the full-blown sails,
  That bring to our shores brave hearts and hands !

Oh ! blow, WEST WIND, with thy fresh, strong breeze,
  Prepare our frames for the frost and snow ;
Shake down the ripe fruits from off the trees,
  And tinge our cheeks with health's ruddy glow !

God tempers the winds for life or death,
  As over the earth they sweeping go ;
He speaks in the zephyr's balmy breath,
  As well as when loudest tempests blow.

AN HONEST MAN.

"An honest man 's the noblest work of God."—*Burns.*

SHEW me the man of true and honest heart,
Who, for the sake of gain, will not depart
From paths of rectitude, and then I can
Shew you God's noblest work—
An honest man!

Temptation's darts do not disturb his mind,
True to himself he 's true to all mankind,
By honest toil he earns whate'er he can,
And proves himself to be—
An honest man!

Truth is his watchword—lips that speak no guile,
His face illumin'd with an honest smile,
Looks eye to eye with ours, nor fails to scan
The traits and signs which mark—
The honest man!

God bless the honest man whose bosom thrills
With love and sympathy for others' ills,
And "robs" himself of ease if so he can,
With woman's tenderness, display—
" The man !"

The world is full of sin, and vice, and crime,
But honesty will stand the test of time;
Truth, Virtue, Charity, shall lead the van,—
God's name is honour'd by—
The honest man!

LIFE'S BRIGHTER SIDE.

'TIS better to smile than to frown,
  'Tis better to laugh than to cry ;
Then, don't let your spirits get down,
  And never say " fail " tho' you die !

Though trouble like mountains arise,
  And fortune seems hard to attain,
Look hopefully up to the skies,
  For sunshine will come after rain.

Those taught in adversity's school
  Are braver and better by far ;
The cowardly man, as a rule,
  Is not to be trusted in war.

A brave heart is sure to succeed,
  The weak one will go to the wall ;
And God will assist those indeed
  Who help themselves up when they fall.

If in love affections are bent,
  And wooing is met with disdain,
Bear up with apparent content,
  And time will restore you again !

The world is more full of joy
  Than most people care to admit ;
If usefully time you'll employ,
  Life's trials won't hurt you a bit !

SOAP-BUBBLES.

WHAT a happy holiday,
Brothers Jack and Will at play;
Blowing bubbles light as air,
Chasing them o'er stool and chair!
As they blow, each ruddy cheek
Happiness and joy bespeak;
Each the other tries to " chaff "—
Hard to blow when forc'd to laugh!

Little " pussy " likes the fun,
Swift across the floor to run,
When they break across her eyes,
Gets " her back up " in surprise!
Tasting soap in mouth and nose,
Sniffing to a corner goes!
Till another tempts her out,
Once again to run about!

Mamma hears the noisy din,
Slyly at the door peeps in;
But she loves to see them play,
Happy in their joy alway!
Swift a thought across her mind
Utterance finds in words so kind :—
Ah ! my boys, a moral see
From the bubbles light and free:

L.

Empty bubbles, light as air,
For a moment bright and fair;
Some ascend like stars to heaven,
Some to swift destruction driven;
If thou would'st escape each snare,
Guard thy life with constant prayer;
God will waft thee to the skies,
Float thee into Paradise!

KNIGHTS OF PYTHIAS.

COME, Knights of Pythias, all combine,
Let Friendship, Truth, and Love entwine;
Our noble deeds, with one accord,
Shall conquests make that shame the sword!

CHORUS.—Come, join together heart and hand,
United we shall ever stand;
Encircle earth by sea and land,
With Friendship's loving golden band!

Our Order stands the test of time,—
A foe to falsehood, want, and crime;
A band of brothers, brave and free,
The "Golden Rule" our only plea!

CHORUS.—"Come join," etc.

The widows' and the orphans' cause
Are part and parcel of our laws;
We help the needy, shield the weak,
And words of sympathy we speak.

CHORUS.—"Come join," etc.

Should dire Oppression's iron hand
Be laid upon our native land,
Our swords shall strike the tyrant low,
And Freedom smile at every blow!

CHORUS.—"Come join," etc.

THE YOUNG MUSICIAN.

Music by Prof. J. F. Johnstone.
Simply.   Toronto.

A, B, C, D, E, F, G, That's the scale as you may see;

On the lines and in the space; Each in or - der you may trace!

CHORUS.

A, B, C, D, E, F, G, A mu - sic - ian I would be;

Oh, it is such mer-ry fun, Up and down the scale to run!

E, F, G, A, B, C, D, E, D, C, B, A, G, F, E,

Oh, it is such mer-ry fun, Up and down the scale to run!

THE YOUNG MUSICIAN.

A—B,—C,—D,—E,—F,—G,
That's "*the scale*," as you may see;
On the "*lines*" and in the "*space*,"
Each in order you may trace!

CHORUS.—A,—B,—C,—D,—E,—F,—G,
A musician I would be;
Oh, it is such merry fun
Up and down "the scale" to run!

E,—G,—B,—D,—F,—on "*lines*,"
Learn by sight the useful signs;
F,—A,—C,—E,—in the "*space*,"
Don't forget the spelling—FACE!

CHORUS.—"A, B, C, D, E, F, G," etc.

Notes are simply "*signs*" you see,
Round and black as black can be;
From the perfect number "*seven*,"
Each its proper place is given!

CHORUS.—"A, B, C, D, E, F, G," etc.

" *Sharps* " and " *flats* " some patience need,
    If at music you'd succeed ;
    But " *sweet melody* " is there,
    When you take great pains and care !
CHORUS.—"A, B, C, D, E, F, G," etc.

    Soon my little friend may try
    Something greater by-and-by,
    If her teacher she obeys,
    And remembers all he says !
CHORUS.—"A, B, C, D, E, F, G," etc.

    Just be patient—never fret,
    Or into a passion get ;
    Else " *a discord* " you will make,
    Which would be " *a great mistake !* "
CHORUS.—"A, B, C, D, E, F, G," etc.

THE YOUNG MUSICIAN.

Just be patient—never fret,
Or into a passion get ;
Else " *a discord* " you will make,
Which would be " *a great mistake !* "

CHORUS.—A,—B,—C,—D,—E,—F,—G,
A musician I would be ;
Oh, it is such merry fun
Up and down " the scale " to run !

THE KNIGHTS OF LABOUR.

A power has risen in the land,
Who work together hand-in-hand,
A noble, energetic band,—
    The Knights of Labour.

Monopoly must not control
The labour market, heart and soul,
And seek to pay with meagre dole
    The Knights of Labour.

Let man to man this maxim tell:
" He doeth right who worketh well,
And ought to best advantage sell
    His wealth of labour !"

Though wealth be strong, yet right is might,
And victory shall crown the right,—
All honour to your noble fight,
    Brave Knights of Labour !

While enterprise we will respect,
Our rights we never shall neglect;
All tyranny we must reject
    While Knights of Labour !

THE WORKINGMAN'S HALF-HOLIDAY.

GOD bless the men of means who try
  To sweeten Labour's cup,
By list'ning to the earnest cry
  To lift "the masses up"
Above the drudgery of life,
  The needful hours to spare,
A short respite from busy strife,
  Sweet Nature's joys to share!

'Twill prove the best investment sure,
  These hours to toilers given,
'Twill tend to make them good and pure,
  And pave their way to Heaven;
Respect and honesty will spring
  From hearts made glad and free,
To duty more attention bring,
  Thy grateful servants be.

And, then, what pleasure to thy heart,
  To mark the happy faces,
As pleasure parties gaily start
  For rural, healthy places,
To breathe the sweet pure air of heaven,
  By mountain, lake or river,
And use the means thus kindly given
  As best would please the giver!

Then give without a grudge or fear
　　The boon so much desired,
The patient wife and children dear
　　With hope shall feel inspired;
Life shall be then worth living for,
　　Dull care shall fly away,
And once a week no cloud shall mar
　　Their glad half-holiday!

THE SUNDAY-SCHOOL INFANT CLASS.

SIXTY little smiling faces,
All in their accustom'd places ;
Each a happy household's treasure,
Teaching them a perfect pleasure.

Sixty pair of eyes, whose gladness
Shews no trace of care or sadness,
Are fix'd on me with glances bright,
Like twinkling orbs of purest light.

Sixty voices in a chorus :
" *Childhood's years are passing o'er us :*"
May those years to God be given,
Walking in the way to Heaven.

Hopeful hearts are rais'd in pray'r,
Craving God's peculiar care ;
Waiting for the children's blessing,
Faith and love their hearts possessing.

Childish words, brimful of trust :
" *Jesus, Thou canst make us just,*"
May we now and ever share
In our Father's watchful care."

How they listen to the story
Of redeeming love and glory :
That Jesus took the sinner's place,
In boundless love and matchless grace.

Simple words and illustration,
Suited to their humble station ;
" Line upon line " they learn to know
The Word of God, and wiser grow.

Their minds, thus stor'd with heavenly truth,
Will fence them from the snares of youth,
And thus a safe foundation lay
To lead them through life's rugged way.

Oh, blessed are the children dear
Who love the Lord, and in His fear
Do walk in His most holy way
That leads to everlasting day !

And blessed is the teacher's part,
To educate the infant heart ;
A Saviour's love to them unfold,
Truths ever new and never old !

THE DYING CHILD.

BESIDE the death-bed of her child
  A mother bent in grief,
But to her pain and anguish wild
  There came a sweet relief.

The dying child, in accents mild,
  And full of tender love,
The silence broke while thus she spoke
  Of brighter scenes above:

"Oh, mother dear, you need not fear
  Nor fret yourself for me,
Dry from your cheek the falling tear,
  I soon shall happy be.

"I soon shall reach that 'happy land,'
  And join that blessed throng,
Who ever stand at God's right hand
  Singing the angels' song.

"I'll wait for you and father dear
  On that bright, happy shore,
Where death nor sorrow cometh near,
  And friends depart no more.

"Then let me go—I must not stay,
 I hear my Saviour's voice;
The angels beckon me away,
 And bid my soul rejoice."

The angels fair have come and gone,
 They bore that child away;
Another soul is at the throne,
 Here but the lifeless clay.

Oh, friends bereaved, weep not for those
 Whom Jesus died to save;
Through Him they conquer'd all their foes
 And triumphed o'er the grave!

CONSECRATION.

NOT my will, but Thine, O Lord!
Trusting to Thy promis'd Word;
Keep me ever near to Thee,
All through life my guardian be.
Teach me all I ought to know,
Guide me where I ought to go,
Be my Comforter and Friend,
Till I reach my journey's end!

Let my heart its fulness tell,
Gratitude my bosom swell;
Patient, humble, mild, and meek,
Let my lips Thy praises speak.
Darkness Thou hast turn'd to day,
Swept my guilty fears away;
Thou art all in all to me,—
I am naught compar'd to Thee!

When at last life's battle o'er,—
Landed safe on Canaan's shore,
I shall see Thy blessed face
Lighten up that glorious place;
Prostrate at Thy feet I'll fall,
There Thy wondrous love recall,—
Love so boundless, deep, and free,
That it compass'd—"EVEN ME!"

HAPPY CHILDHOOD.

HAPPY childhood, full of smiles,
  All the livelong day;
Winsome ways and cunning wiles,
  Ever fond of play.

How our hearts with pleasure beat,
  Feeling young and gay;
When we see them on the street,
  Sadness flies away!

Care or sorrow hath no part
  In life's early day,
Thine the light and happy heart,
  Singing merrily!

Like the flowers of early Spring
  O'er the meadows cast,
Sweetness to our hearts they bring,
  Dear mem'ries of the past.

But the future, who can tell
  What their lot may be?
God, who doeth all things well,
  Keep them pure and free!

ON MY FORTIETH BIRTHDAY.

FORTY years of age to-day !
Ah ! how time doth pass away ;
Like a pleasant summer's day,
Or like children's hours of play !

Now I've reach'd ripe manhood's prime,
Fain would bar the march of time ;
Raven locks now tipp'd with grey,
Show the signs of sure decay.

Grateful love my heart doth fill,—
Reach'd the summit of life's hill ;
Safe through many an anxicus care,
" *Thank Thee, Lord*," my daily prayer.

Now a-down " life's other side,"
Knowing not what may betide ;
Trusting where I cannot trace,
Till I see God face to face !

Let the years, then, come and go,
Fraught with weal or mix'd with woe ;
I will trust my Father's love
Till I reach His home above !

THE "LOVES" OF AN INFANT-CLASS SCHOLAR.

I love to hear the school-bell ring,
I love to hear the children sing;
I love to see the house of pray'r,
I love to *know* that God is there.

I love to see my teacher's face,
All beaming with a heavenly grace;
I love to make my teacher glad,
When naughty children make her sad.

I love to read my Bible true,
I love my Father's will to do;
I love to *feel* my sins forgiv'n,
I love to think of God and Heav'n.

I love to learn the heavenly way,
In Sabbath-school—on Sabbath day;
I love to bring my playmates there,
I love my lessons to prepare.

I love my mother—oh, so dear!
I love my father's heart to cheer;
I love my brothers, kind and true,
I love my own dear sisters too.

M

I love to think of Jesus mild,
And how *He loves* a little child;
I love to know that "GOD IS LOVE,"
And smiles on *me* from Heav'n above.

I love to think that when I die
God waits for me beyond the sky;
And when I reach that "happy land,"
I'll walk with Jesus *hand-in-hand!*

PRIDE.

PRIDE is Satan's favourite plant,
   A noxious weed infernal ;
A passion-flower of waste and want,
   To poison souls eternal !

How foolish is the pride of man,
   The creature of a day,
Whose life is measur'd by a span,
   And then returns to clay !

When first our eyes beheld the light
   No claim to pomp had we ;
All men are equal in God's sight,
   Sustain'd, belov'd, and free !

Our Saviour died for all mankind,
   A full and free salvation ;
Then why should we be so unkind,
   As sneer at dress or station ?

The Son of God had humble birth,
   Yet now He reigns in Heaven ;
Those who oppress the poor on earth
   Shall from His throne be driven !

THE ABSENT SUNDAY-SCHOOL TEACHER.

OH ! children dear,
　She is not here,
Your teacher loving and true ;
　But gone above,
　Where all is love,
Waiting and watching for you.

　For you her tears,
　And pray'rs, and fears,
Will not have been spent in vain ;
　If lessons taught
　Are not forgot,
You shall meet with her again !

　In that bright land,
　At God's right hand,
Where Jesus shall claim His own,—
　With smiling face,
　Appoint a place
Around His glorious throne.

　Oh ! happy land,
　Thrice happy band,
Beside the shining river ;
　In Jesus' praise
　Your voices raise
In songs that last for ever !

THE BITTER OR THE SWEET.

THE bitter or the sweet of life
   Is often ours to choose,
Sweet ove is antidote to strife—
   The bitter, then, refuse.

Let not the angry word be said,
   At home, at work, or play;
Like waters pure from fountain-head
   Let smiles cheer up thy way.

Let Mara's bitter waters flow
   Alone on deserts wild;
On life's highway, whereon we go,
   Let looks and words be mild.

Let wreaths of smiles chase every frown
   From God's own image fair;
Then friendsliip's loving hands shall crown
   Thy head with blessings rare.

Now, all along life's rugged way
   Let flowers displace the thorn,
And grief and care shall flee away
   From hearts that erst were torn!

LOVE AND SYMPATHY.

THE balm of sympathy how sweet
   In trial's pensive hour,
When wave on wave of sorrows beat,
   And clouds of darkness lower.

'Tis then that Friendship's gentle hand
   May half our burden share;
'Tis then we fully understand
   The love to us they bear.

Oh! Love and Sympathy how dear
   To those bow'd down with care;
Thy angel-face dispels our fear,
   Makes hearts feel light as air.

Though Ophir's wealth were wholly mine,
   All jewels rich and rare,
For love of friends I yet would pine,
   And find my treasure there.

Our first experience at birth
   Was sympathy and love,
And when at last we leave this earth
   We'll find its Source above.

THE BROTHERHOOD OF MAN.

OUR Father—God, His children—we,
No matter where our birthplace be—
'Mid Arctic snows, or torrid clime,
One family since the first of time!

We should not bind our fellow-man,
Though he be yellow, black, or tan;
Or seek to keep him trodden down
By haughty sneer, or cruel frown.

A mother's love, like that of Heav'n,
Alike to all her sons is giv'n,—
All men are free as God's pure air,
And all alike His image bear.

Far better we should ever try
To ease the load, or soothe the sigh;
Each other's burdens kindly bear,
Each other's joys or sorrows share!

How can we pray to God above,
And daily seek His care and love,
Unless our hearts for others' woe
With sympathetic love o'erflow?

ON A VISIT TO THE "OLD COUNTRY."

ACROSS the wide Atlantic sea
   Our steamer speeds her way,
Great billows rolling grand and free
   Rest not by night or day.

At last the land recedes from sight,—
   The great new land of hope,
Where enterprise and honest might
   Find fair and ample scope.

A week has pass'd, yet sea and sky
   Seem all of earth to me,
Until at last the welcome cry
   Is heard with joy and glee :—

" Land, ho !—land, ho ! "—a sailor cries,
   But naught to us is seen ;
An hour or two, and then our eyes
   Behold the welcome scene :—

Great headlands rise, like sentries bold,
   Or guardians of the land ;
Their tops, like helmets, shine with gold
   In sunset hues so grand !

Still on we speed, with hope and joy
   Our hearts feel like to sing !
Our thoughts on "home" find sweet employ
   As early scenes up-spring !

The fair green hills of Ireland rise,
  Resplendent to the view,
And seem an earthly Paradise
  To loving hearts and true!

'Tis hard to leave the deck to-night,
  I scarce can go to sleep;
I toss and dream, till morning light
  Comes shining o'er the deep!

Now, dear old Scotia's mountains rise
  As up the Clyde we steam,
Like friends of old they cheer our eyes,
  Or like a pleasant dream!

At last we reach the same old pier
  Where years ago we parted,
Here once we wept, now joy's glad tear
  From loving eyes have started!

Oh, friends of early days, and "home"
  Of childhood's happy years;
My thoughts are yours where'er I roam,
  For you my prayers and tears!

" FAREWELL ! "

THE saddest word we ever hear,
Full-fraught with sorrow, hope, and fear,
The fount of many a bitter tear:
  Farewell ! Farewell !

REFRAIN : Farewell ! Farewell !
        Ah ! who can tell
          What bitter tears,
          What hopes and fears,
        Surround thy spell ?
        Sad word : " Farewell ! "

As, branch by branch, the family tree
Is snapp'd and floated o'er life's sea,
How sad a parent's heart must be,
  To say : " Farewell ! "

REFRAIN : " Farewell ! Farewell ! " etc.

How sad for loving friends to part
For distant scenes—so wide apart—
That mem'ries must suffice the heart
  That says : " Farewell ! "

REFRAIN : " Farewell ! Farewell ! " etc.

How sad to hear the deep-toned bell
Ring out a dear friend's funeral knell,
And feel your very heart-strings swell
   To say : " Farewell ! "

REFRAIN : " Farewell ! Farewell ! " etc.

When we have said our last " Farewell,"
And gone the ranks of heaven to swell,
Rejoice to know—Death breaks the spell—
   All's well ! all's well !

REFRAIN : With God to dwell,
     No more, " Farewell ! "
       No more sad tears !
       No doubts ! no fears !
     Each tongue shall tell :
   " 'Tis well ! 'Tis well ! "

FRAGMENTS FOR AUTOGRAPH ALBUMS.

———

A FEW short years
Of hopes and fears,
And then we pass for ever
Where answer'd prayers
Shall banish cares,
Beyond the shining river !

Blest land above,
Sweet home of love,
With joy we'll reach thy portals ;
'Mid angel throngs,
Recite the songs
Sung by redeem'd immortals !

———

THE friendship of the good and true
Is more to me than gold,
And while I welcome one that's new
I'll treasure well the old ;
Old friends are like the goodly tree
Whose leafy branches throw
A grateful shelter over me
When adverse winds may blow !

ALPHABETICAL INDEX.

—